THE ARABIAN NIGHTS

CHILDREN'S
CLASSICS

THE ARABIAN NIGHTS

Bloomsbury Books
London

This edition published 1994 by Bloomsbury Books, an
imprint of The Godfrey Cave Group, 42 Bloomsbury Street,
London, WC1B 3QJ.

ISBN 1 85471 266 7

Printed and bound by Firmin-Didot (France),
Group Herissey. No d'impression : 26803.

Contents

Sindbad the Sailor

During the reign of the Caliph Haroun Alraschid there lived in the city of Bagdad a poor porter named Hindbad, who had to toil very hard in order to earn a wretched living.

One hot summer's day he was given a heavy burden to carry from one end of the city to the other, and feeling very tired, upon reaching a certain quiet street, where a gentle breeze was blowing and rose-water was sprinkled on the pavement, he sat down to rest for a while against the walls of a great house.

A grand feast was going on within, and the merry sounds of a concert of music soon reached the ears of the porter, and wishing to know to whom the house belonged, he went up to a slave who stood at the gate, and asked the name of his master.

"What!" cried the slave, "you live in Bagdad, and yet don't know that this is the house of the famous Sindbad the Sailor, who has travelled all over the world!"

Now, Hindbad had often heard of this Sindbad, who was one of the richest men in Bagdad, and feeling envious of the great sailor, as he compared his good fortune with his own wretchedness, he could not help crying out aloud:

"Oh, what a difference between happy Sindbad and wretched Hindbad! I have to toil hard every day, and can scarcely earn bread for my family; but he has all that money can buy, and lives a life of constant pleasure! What has Sindbad done to descrve such happiness, and what have I done that I should remain so wretched?"

In saying this, he stamped the ground with his foot, as if he had given up everything in despair.

Now, this complaint was heard by those within the house, and presently a slave came out to take Hindbad before his master.

It may easily be imagined that Hindbad was, indeed, very much surprised at the compliment that was paid him. After the words that he had used, he began to fear that Sindbad had sent for him so that he could punish him, and therefore he tried to excuse himself from going, saying that he could not leave his load in the middle of the street; but the servant, assuring him that it should be taken care of, pressed him so much to go that the porter could no longer refuse.

He was led into the great hall of the house, where a splendid feast was being held, and a large number of gaily dressed guests were sitting round a table covered with rich dishes.

At one end of the table sat a pleasant-looking man, whose long white beard showed that he was getting on in years, and round about him stood a number of slaves ready to carry out his commands. This was the famous Sindbad, the giver of the feast; and still fearing that his hasty words had offended the great sailor, Hindbad trembled as he humbly paid his respects to him and to the rest of the company.

However, he need have had no fear, for Sindbad received him very kindly, and made him sit down at his right hand and enjoy the feast. When the astonished porter had made a good meal, Sindbad said to him:

"My friend, I heard your complaint just now, but do not blame you. Yet you make a mistake if you imagine I reached my present happiness without much trouble and suffering for many years. If my guests are willing, I will now tell you the story of my seven voyages, that you may know I speak the truth."

The guests were all ready enough to listen to the great

sailor's adventures; and so, having ordered a slave to carry the porter's burden to the place he named, Sindbad began the story of his first voyage.

SINDBAD'S FIRST VOYAGE

"When my father died he left me a good fortune, which I enjoyed for some time; but a great love of adventure soon made me give up my easy life and take to the sea.

"I threw in my lot with some roving merchants, and, having fitted out a ship for trading purposes, we set sail for the Indian seas, stopping at various islands to buy or to sell goods.

"One day we stopped near a small island to wait for a breeze to take us ahead, and as some of the party wished to land, I went with them. But imagine our terror when, as soon as we had made a fire to cook our food, the island suddenly began to tremble and quake most horribly!

"The shaking of the island was seen by those on board ship, and the captain quickly shouted to us to return at once, since what we had taken for an island was really only the back of a gigantic whale.

"There was a wild rush for the boats at once, but before I could get away, the monster dived into the sea, tossing me into the waves, and by the time I rose again I found that the ship had sailed away, the captain having thought me drowned.

"I clung to a piece of wood I managed to seize, and after struggling with the waves for many hours, I was at length flung upon the shores of an island.

"I rested for a while, and after refreshing myself with some wild fruits I walked forward into the island. I went on till I came to an open plain, where I found a horse feeding.

"I was admiring the horse, when a man came up and demanded to know what I was doing there. I told him my story, and then he led me to a cave, where a number of other men were gathered together.

"They gave me some food, and whilst I was eating they

told me that they were grooms to the great King Mihrage who ruled over the island, and were now travelling to his palace with the fine horse I had seen.

"Next day they went on with their journey, taking me with them; and when we arrived at the capital they took me to the palace and presented me to King Mihrage, who received me very kindly. He asked me many questions, and when I had finished the story of my adventure, he said I should be well cared for so long as I remained in his country, and gave orders to his attendants to see that I wanted for nothing.

"I determined to make the best use of my time in this island, so visited the merchants and learnt much of their ways of trading; and I also talked frequently with the learned Indians, who spent all their lives in studying and seeking out hidden knowledge.

"Nor did I neglect to pay my respects every day to the king and his viziers, who all took very great pleasure in asking me questions about the laws and customs of my own country.

"I went one day to see a wonderful island belonging to King Mihrage, which was named Cassel, and which the sailors declared was the abode of Degial, the spirit of evil, since a mystic sound of drums was to be heard there every night; and on the way to this island I saw fish from sixty to a hundred and twenty yards long, and other fish that had heads like owls.

"King Mihrage's capital lay on the coast, and had a splendid harbour, where ships arrived every day from all parts of the world; and one morning, as I stood watching the unloading of some bales from a newly-arrived vessel, I saw, to my surprise, that these goods were marked with my own name.

"I then went on board, and found that the captain was indeed the one with whom I had set sail. He was delighted to see me again, and to know that I had escaped drowning after all; and I soon made up my mind to return home with him.

"I took a handsome present from my bales to King

Mihrage, telling him how I had met with my merchant friend again; and, after thanking him for his kindness to me, I bade him farewell.

"The king was much pleased with my present, and also made me a more valuable gift in return; and then, having taken on board a quantity of precious woods and spices, I set sail once more.

"We passed several islands, where we sold or exchanged our goods, and at last we arrived in Balsora, where I landed with the fine sum of a hundred thousand sequins.

"I hurried on to Bagdad; and, having bought a splendid house, I gave money away to the poor, and settled down to enjoy my good fortune."

Sindbad stopped his story here, and, sending for a purse of a hundred sequins, he gave it to Hindbad, and invited him to come to another feast next day, when he should hear more of his adventures. The delighted porter hurried home to tell the good news to his family, and next day he returned at the same time to Sindbad's house, dressed in his best clothes. Another feast was being held; and as soon as Hindbad and the other guests had finished, Sindbad began the story of his second voyage.

SINDBAD'S SECOND VOYAGE

"I had determined, after my first voyage, to pass the rest of my days in peace and quietness at Bagdad. But I soon grew tired of my idle life, and, desirous of seeing foreign countries, I went to sea again with another party of merchants.

"We did a brisk trade from island to island, and soon added greatly to our fortunes.

"One day we landed on a desert island to refresh ourselves with the delicious fruits we saw there, and, as I afterwards felt rather tired, I lay down alone in a quiet spot to sleep. When I awoke I found to my horror that the ship had sailed without me, and that I was left alone upon a desert island, with no chance of escaping from it, since it was not a place where ships were likely to call.

"At first I was full of despair at my sad lot; but after a while, knowing that sighs were of no avail, I began to look about me.

"I soon noticed a huge, white object lying at a little distance, and, making my way towards it, I found that it was a dome as smooth as polished ivory, and at least fifty paces round. I walked round to see whether there was an opening, but I could find none. I tried to climb it, but only slipped back each time; and, as I stood gazing upon it, I noticed that the sky was suddenly growing dark, as though covered with a dense black cloud.

"I soon saw, to my astonishment, that this blackness was caused by a monstrous bird flying down towards me. I had often heard sailors speak of a giant bird called a roc; and I made up my mind that this terrible creature flying towards me was one, and that the great white dome beside me was its egg.

"Seeing in this monster a means of escape for me, I crept as closely as I could get to the white dome, so that when the giant bird alighted, and sat on her egg, she covered me also with her great wings. I then tied myself firmly with my turban to one of her legs, which was as thick as the trunk of a tree, and when she arose next morning into the sky she carried me away with her.

"When she had risen to a great height she came down so suddenly that I fainted; but when she reached the ground I recovered, and unfastened myself at once. I had only just set myself free when the roc, having snatched up in her bill an enormous serpent, to serve her as a worm flew away.

"I found that I had been left in a very deep valley rounded on every side by such vast rocky mountains that it was impossible to climb them, and so I was no better off than before. As I walked along this valley I found that it was strewn with diamonds of the largest and most dazzling kind, and since I had nothing better to do I filled all my pockets and loose clothing with them.

"I also saw a swarm of dreadful serpents, a sight which

filled me with terror. These serpents were so long and large that the smallest of them was huge enough to have easily swallowed an elephant. To my relief, I found that they remained in their dens throughout the day to hide from the roc, and only came out at night.

"I wandered about all day in this beautiful valley of diamonds, and when night came I crept into a cave, and blocked up the opening with stones, that I might be safe from the terrible serpents, which I soon heard swarming and hissing outside.

"In the morning the serpents returned to their dens for safety from the roc, and then I came out of my cave. Later in the day I was much surprised to see; that great pieces of raw meat were being thrown down into the valley, but I soon understood what this meant.

"I had often heard of a famous valley of diamonds, where, though it is impossible to go down into it, the merchants manage to get some of the precious stones by means of a cunning trick. From the rocks above they throw great joints of raw meat into the Diamond Valley. These pieces of meat fall upon the sharp points of the gems, which sticks to them. By and by the eagles, which are larger and stronger there than in any other parts of the world, pounce upon the pieces of meat and carry them away to their nests on the tops of the rocks, to feed their young ones with; and then the merchants frighten the eagles away, and pick out the diamonds that stick to the meat.

"I had never believed this story until now, when I found myself actually in this very valley of diamonds.

"I had thought that it would be quite impossible for me to get out of this wonderful valley, and I had begun to look upon it as being my grave. But the pieces of meat falling around me soon led me to plan out a way of escape from my prison.

"I first of all filled a bag I had with me as full as it would hold with the largest diamonds I could find, and took one of the pieces of meat and fastened it firmly to my back with

my turban. Then I laid myself face downwards on the
ground, and waited for the eagles to come.

"I had not long to wait, for presently one of the strongest
eagles caught me up by the piece of meat I had tied to my
back, and flew away with me to a nest on the mountain-top.

"The merchants began to frighten away the birds and ran
immediately to get their treasures. Very soon one of them
came to the nest where I lay.

"He was astonished to see me, and at first was angry,
thinking I had come to steal his diamonds, but when I had
told him my story he was ready enough to believe me.

"The other merchants now came crowding round; and,
when I had also told my story to them, they received me
very kindly, and took me to the place where they had
pitched their tents. Here I showed them my diamonds, and
all declared they had never before seen gems so large and
dazzling. I begged the merchant who had found me to help
himself to some of my treasures, but I could only persuade
him to take one, which he said was large enough to gain
him a large fortune.

"Next morning the merchants, having thrown their raw
meat into the valley for some time, declared themselves satisfied with the diamonds they had obtained; and so we left
that place, and started on our journey home, I throwing in
my lot with my new friends.

"We passed over high mountains, where we saw more
serpents of tremendous length, which filled us with terror,
but from which we were fortunate enough to escape; and,
taking ship at the first port we came to, we at last arrived
safely at Balsora.

"I soon made my way to Bagdad with the vast treasures
which I had gained; and having given away large presents
to the poor, I began to live upon my riches in splendid
style."

Sindbad, having ended the story of his second voyage,
gave the delighted porter another hundred sequins, and invited him to come again next day to hear about his third

voyage. You may be sure Hindbad did not forget to come; and, when the guests had all feasted, Sindbad went on with his story.

SINDBAD'S THIRD VOYAGE

"The happy life that I had spent since my last voyage had made me forget all the dangers I had gone through, but as I was young and strong I again got tired of my lazy life.

"It was not long, therefore, before I set sail once again with another party of merchants, to seek adventures and treasures. We made a long voyage, trading at the various places we came to; but one day we were caught in a terrible storm, which drove us out of our way.

"We drifted along for some days; and then, as the storm continued, we were obliged to enter the harbour of a certain island, where the captain was very unwilling to take shelter. He told us that in all the islands about here there were hosts of wild savages, who, although but dwarfs, would soon overcome us, and if we dared to kill but one of them, they would destroy us all; and what he said proved only too true.

"Presently a swarm of the most frightful savages came swimming towards us, and clambered into the ship. They were covered with red hair, and, though the largest was not more than two feet in height, they were so fierce, and came in such vast numbers, that we could not keep them back. We dared not harm them, and in a very short time they unfurled the sails, cut the cable from the anchor, and made us get on shore. They then hauled our ship away to another island, from which they had come.

"We soon found out that the island where we had been left was a very dangerous one, and was always avoided by all ships that passed that way, for a reason of which I will tell you presently.

"We left the shore and walked into the island a little way, where we found some fruits and herbs, which we ate, and soon came to a huge palace, larger than any we had ever seen before. We entered through the gateway, and found ourselves in a large hall, on the one side of which, to our horror, was a great heap of human bones, and on the other a number of spits for roasting.

"Whilst we were trembling at this fearful sight, there suddenly came into the room a horrible black giant, who was as tall as a palm-tree, and had but one great eye, like a red burning coal. This eye stood in the middle of his forehead. His long, sharp teeth projected from his mouth like tusks, his ears hung down over his shoulders, his nails were long and curved like the talons of a huge bird, and he was altogether such a dreadful-looking monster that we all lost our senses at the sight of him, and lay on the floor like dead men.

"When we opened our eyes once more, the ogre was still looking at us; but presently he seized the captain, who was the fattest of our number, and, holding him in his hand as though he were a sparrow, he thrust a spit through him. He then made a great fire, and roasted and ate him for his supper, and when he had finished he lay down and fell asleep, his snoring sounding like the rolling of thunder. Next morning, when he awoke, he went out and left us alone.

"You can imagine the terror we were all in; indeed our fear was so great that at first we were powerless to think out a plan of escape. We spent the day wandering about the island in search of fruits and herbs for food; and when night came we were forced to return to the palace, since we could find no other place of shelter. The ogre soon appeared, and having again supped upon another of our companions, he lay down and slept until morning, when he arose and left us.

"This went on for several days; but at last I suggested that we should try to make some rafts and escape by sea. We found plenty of wood about the shore, and when the rafts were ready we returned to the palace for the last time.

"The ogre came as usual, and, having eaten another of our party for his supper, lay down and fell asleep; but this time we found courage to take revenge on him. Each one of us that were left seized spits, and making them red-hot in the fire, we thrust them all at once into the giant's great eye, and blinded him. He sprang up with a terrific yell, and rushed out of the castle, howling with pain.

"Directly he had gone, we all rushed down to the shore, and launched our rafts; but no sooner had we got on board than the ogre appeared again, with several other giants as large and dreadful as himself. We got away from the shore as quickly as possible; but the monsters came striding into the sea after us, and, taking up great stones, they threw them at us with great force.

"Unhappily they aimed so well that they sank all the rafts except the one on which I was seated with two others, and we were the only ones who escaped drowning.

"We rowed with all our might until we got out of reach of the giants, and, after being tossed about for a long while by the seas, our raft was at length thrown upon an island.

"We passed the night upon the shore, but were rudely awakened by a loud noise caused by the rustling of a fearful serpent as long as a palm-tree. It swallowed one of my companions, and, full of terror, the two of us that were left fled away to a great distance, groaning at the dangers to which we were constantly exposed.

"Next day we saw the serpent again, and though at night we climbed up into a tall tree for safety, it found us out, and, wriggling up the trunk, swallowed my companion, who sat lower than I. It then went away, and next morning I came down from the tree and made a great circle of brambles and thorn bushes all around my hiding-place.

"I climbed back to my perch, and when evening came the serpent returned, but was not able to get through the circle of wood I had made. He crawled and hissed outside all night, and did not leave me till day. I waited a little longer, and then, coming down from the tree, I rushed towards the sea, meaning to throw myself in, since I could bear my troubles no longer.

"Just as I was about to throw myself amidst the waves, I saw, to my joy, a ship not far out, and by wildly waving my hands I managed to attract the notice of the captain, who quickly sent a boat to fetch me on board. On hearing my story, the captain received me kindly, giving me food, and bidding me rest. Seeing that I was in rags, he also gave me some of his own clothes. I found that those on board were merchants, and we traded at all the places we came to.

"One day the captain came to me, and, putting some bales of goods into my charge, asked me to arrange the sale of them for him, saying he would pay me well for my trouble. I gladly accepted his offer, not caring to be idle amongst so many busy people; but great was my astonishment when I found that the bales were entered in the name of Sindbad.

"Going up to the captain I now recognized him as the one with whom I had set sail on my second voyage, and upon my asking him about the man to whom the bales had belonged, he said: ' They belonged to a merchant named Sindbad, who, having landed on a desert island, did not return with the others. We did not notice his absence until four hours later, and then it was not possible for us to return for him, since we were caught in a gale?"

"You think him dead, then?" I asked.

"Certainly!" replied the captain. I then looked at him steadily, and said: "No, captain, he is not dead; for you behold in me that same Sindbad, who was left upon the desert island!" The captain now recognized me; and, embracing me with great joy, he restored to me my bales of goods.

"We sailed from island to island, buying and selling spices and precious woods, and many were the curious creatures with which we met on our way. One time we saw a tortoise about twelve yards in length and breadth; and another time I caught sight of a sea-beast which was the size and shape of a camel.

"At last, after a long and prosperous voyage, we returned to Balsora, and I arrived in Bagdad with such great riches that I knew not their value."

When Sindbad had finished this story, he gave Hindbad another hundred sequins, and told him to come next day to feast, and hear more of his adventures. The porter gladly did so, and when the feast was over, Sindbad began the story of his fourth voyage.

SINDBAD'S FOURTH VOYAGE

"The very happy time that I spent after my third voyage did not prevent me from venturing out to sea again. So I gave way to my love of adventure, and, having bought goods for trading, I went on board another merchant ship.

"We had not been long at sea, however, when we were caught in a sudden gale, and our ship soon struck on a rock, and most of those on board were drowned. I, together with a few of the merchants and the sailors, managed to cling to pieces of the wreck, and, after struggling with the waves for a long while, we were all drawn by the force of the current towards an island that lay before us.

"Here we were soon seized by some natives, who took us to their huts and shared us amongst them. They made us sit down, and soon gave us a certain herb to eat. I noticed that none of the natives touched this herb themselves, so I would not take any either; but my companions, thinking only of their present hunger, ate greedily of it. I soon saw that the herb had indeed been given us for a purpose, for in a very short time my friends lost their senses, and knew not what they said or did. The natives then gave us rice cooked with cocoanut oil, but I only ate a very little of this.

"I now knew that the natives were cannibals, who gave their victims a herb to deaden their senses, that they might not know the fate in store for them, and afterwards fattened them with rice, and I was glad I had refused to eat the herb, so that I still knew what I was about.

"My poor companions were soon fattened and eaten by the cannibals; but seeing that I kept thin, they left me alone, and after a while I managed to escape from them.

"I wandered about for eight days, when I drew near to the sea again, and presently I came across people like myself, who were gathering pepper, which was very plentiful in that part. I went up to them, and was delighted to find that they understood me when I spoke to them.

"I told them the story of my adventure with the cannibals, and they rejoiced with me in the escape I had had. When they had finished their pepper gathering, they took me away with them to their own island, and presented me to their king, who received me with much honour. He was greatly interested in my story, and, inviting me to stay at his court, he gave orders that I should be well cared for.

"I learnt much from these people, but I was greatly surprised to find that they all rode their horses without saddles, bridles, or stirrups, and had never even heard of such things. I soon set to work, with a slave to help me, to make a saddle, and when it was done I covered it with velvet and gold and presented it to the king, together with a bit and stirrups I had also caused to be made.

"The king was delighted with his gifts, when I showed him how to make use of them; and as all his lords wished me to make such harness for them also I was kept hard at work, and soon grew rich with the money they paid me for my trouble.

"One day, when I went to visit the king as usual, he told me to my surprise and dismay that he had arranged a marriage for me with one of the chief ladies of his court; and, as I dared not refuse the honour thus thrust upon me, I was very shortly afterwards married to this lady. My wife, however, soon became ill and died, and then I found myself in a most horrible fix.

"It was the custom of that place for the living husband to be buried with the dead wife, and the living wife with the dead husband; so no sooner did my wife die than I was ordered to be buried alive with her, and though I begged hard for mercy, being a stranger, none was shown me.

"The burial-place of the island was a cave at the top of the mountain, and the king and all his court came to pay me the last honours.

"When we arrived at the top of the pit, my dead wife, dressed in her most gorgeous robes and dazzling jewels, was lowered in an open coffin to the bottom of the cave, and then my own turn came. My tears and pleadings were all in vain, and I was quickly placed in an open coffin and lowered into the cave, together with a jug of water and seven little loaves to keep me alive a short time longer. The top of the cave was then covered over with a huge stone, and I was left to starve slowly to death.

"Now, I did not mean to die, if I could possibly find some means of saving my life; so I slipped out of my open coffin, and tried to grope my way about. But the cave was so dark I could not find any means of escape, so I returned to my coffin and ate some of my food.

"I lived in this horrible place for several days, and then, when I had eaten the last of my bread, I prepared to die.

"Just then, however, I caught the sound of something panting and moving at the other side of the cave, and, full of hope, I followed this sound as well as I could in the darkness. As I drew nearer, the thing puffed and panted harder than ever, as though running away from me; but I followed it steadily for a long time, till at last I could see a light in the distance. I went on eagerly, and soon found that the light came from a hole in the rock, large enough for a man to get through. I scrambled through the hole as quickly as I could, and, to my great joy, found myself upon the seashore; and then I discovered that the sounds which I had followed were caused by the panting of a creature that came out of the sea to prowl about the cave.

"After I had rested and rejoiced at my escape, I went back to the cave and collected all the jewels and rich stuffs I could find in the coffins, and, having brought these to the shore, I made them up into bales, and then waited for a ship to come by. I had not long to wait, for a merchant vessel soon came past, and, hearing my cries, the captain sent a boat to fetch me. Thinking that some of the people in the ship might belong to the island I had left, I made up a story

about having been shipwrecked and cast ashore with the goods
they saw. The captain was ready enough to believe this story,
and he took me on board at once with all my bales, even refus-
ing to take the jewels I offered him as payment.

"We visited several interesting islands, where we did
good trade, and after a long voyage I at last arrived in
Bagdad.

"In my thankfulness for my happy return I gave splendid
gifts to the mosques, and spent large sums of money for the
support of the poor, and then I once more gave myself up to
enjoyment with my friends."

Sindbad stopped here, and giving the porter another purse
of a hundred sequins, he invited him to come the following
day and hear the story of his fifth voyage.

Hindbad did not fail to come, and when he and the other
guests had feasted, Sindbad went on with his story.

SINDBAD'S FIFTH VOYAGE

"The dangers that I had gone through did not cure me of my
love of travel, and in a very short time I bought goods and
went off to sea again, in a ship of my own this time, together with some merchants I had invited to go with me.

"We made a long voyage, and the first place we stopped
at was a desert island. Here we found a roc's egg, as large as
the one I had seen on my second voyage, and, seeing that it
was just ready to be hatched, my companions, in spite of
my warning, broke open the egg with their axes.

"They then pulled the young roc out, and, making a fire,
they roasted and ate it.

"They had hardly finished their feast when the two parent
rocs appeared in the sky, and in much fear we all returned in
haste to the ship and set sail. The two rocs drew near with a
great noise, and seemed to be in a frightful rage when they
saw that their young one had gone.

"Presently we saw them flying towards us, carrying great
stones, or rather rocks, in their fearful claws. They hovered

just over the ship, and then one of them let fall a stone, which, however, missed the ship and fell into the sea, which dashed up like a great wall of water. But the other roc, unhappily, aimed better, and dropping his enormous stone into the very middle of the ship, splintered her into a thousand pieces.

"I was the only one to escape drowning, and after being tossed about by the waves for some time I was at last able to reach the shores of an island not far away. I found plenty of fruit to eat, and having refreshed myself I lay down and fell asleep.

"Next day, as I walked about under the trees, I came across a wild-looking old man who was sitting on the bank of a stream and was looking weak and, helpless. I greeted him in much surprise, but he only bowed his head in reply to my greeting.

"I then asked why he sat there so still; but, instead of answering, he made me a sign to lift him on to my back and carry him across the brook.

"Thinking he really needed such help, I willingly took him up, and having carried him safely to the other side of the stream I stooped, waiting for him to get down. But instead of this the wretched old creature, who was by no means a weakling as I had supposed, suddenly clasped his legs firmly round my neck, and sitting astride my shoulders he squeezed me so tightly that, in great fear that he would strangle me, I fell down in a faint. When I came round, and had got back my breath, I found the terrible old man still clinging round my neck, and presently he began to kick me so roughly that I was obliged to get up, against my will. He then forced me to walk up and down under the trees, making me stop every now and again to gather such fruits as we found. He never left me all day and at night, and when I was too tired to go another step, and lay down to rest, he would lay himself down beside me and still keep his arms tightly clasped round my neck.

"Next morning he made me get up and carry him again,

and for many days after he forced me to do the same, never leaving me for a moment. I saw that the wicked old creature meant to kill me in time, but at last I found out a way to get rid of my dreadful burden. I squeezed some grapejuice into an empty gourd-shell one morning as I stopped to gather the fruit, which was very plentiful in that place, and coming to it some days later I found that it was already very good wine.

"I drank some of it, and, seeing that it greatly refreshed me, the old man made me a sign to give him some. I gladly did so, seeing in this a means of escape for me. The old fellow liked the wine so well that he drank it all off at once, and I was glad to see that it soon made him so lively and careless that he began to sing and jump about on my shoulders.

"In a short time he loosened his arms from about my neck, so that I was at last able to throw him to the ground, and quickly seizing a great stone I crushed the life out of him.

"Full of joy that I had managed to get rid of this tiresome old wretch, I hurried down to the beach, where I was fortunate enough to meet with some sailors who had landed to take in water for their ship. They were astonished to see me, and when I had told them of my horrid adventure, they said that I had had a very narrow escape, since I had fallen into the clutches of the famous Old Man of the Sea, who never let go of his victims till he had strangled them.

"They then took me to their ship, where I was well received by the captain, who was glad to hear that I had overcome the Old Man of the Sea.

"We soon landed on another island, and here I began to trade in cocoanuts with some other merchants. We went to a great forest of cocoanuts palms, which grew so tall that we could not possibly climb them to get at the fruit; and here we saw more apes and monkeys than I had ever seen before in all my life. The merchants I had joined began to throw stones at the monkeys in the trees, and monkeys, full of rage, pulled the cocoanuts from branches and threw them down at us in revenge.

"We gathered up the cocoanuts at once, and in this manner

we were soon able to fill the bags we had brought with us.

"By going to this forest every day, and selling the cocoanuts which I got from the monkeys, I grew very rich once more; and at last I was able to take a great store on board a merchant ship that called at the island, and trade at the other islands round about. I exchanged my nuts for spices, pearls, and other things of value, and after doing a good trade and gaining great riches I set sail for Balsora.

"When I arrived in Bagdad I made a vast sum of money by the sale of my pearls and other goods, and after having given away valuable presents to the poor, according to my usual custom, I was glad to settle down to rest and pleasure once again."

Having finished this story Sindbad sent the porter away with another hundred sequins, begging him to come again the morrow; and next day, when Hindbad had enjoyed the usual feast, he began the story of his sixth voyage.

SINDBAD'S SIXTH VOYAGE

"I had only been at home one short year, when, weary of such a peaceful life, I made up my mind to go to sea again in search of adventures. This time I went a longer voyage than I had ever undertaken before, and we met with such stormy weather that for a long time we were driven out of our way altogether.

"At last, however, the captain suddenly found out where we were, and then, full of dismay and fear, he tore off his turban and cried out like a madman. We asked him why he acted in this manner, and he replied that we were caught in a most dangerous current of the sea, a current which was so terribly rapid that in less than a quarter of an hour it would carry the ship along with it and would dash her against the rocks.

"We found this to be but too true. The ship was being carried along at a terrific rate, and in a few minutes she was dashed to pieces at the foot of a great rocky mountain.

"We managed, however, to save our lives, and also the greater part of our goods and food; but we soon saw it was impossible for us ever to escape from that dreadful shore. The frightful current that had brought us along so quickly would prevent us from sailing away, even if we had a boat, since it came with such force towards the shore that there was no fighting against it; and the great mountain on the coast rose to such a dreadful height, and was so rocky and steep that it would have been madness to attempt to climb it.

"So we were completely shut in by the sea in front and the mountain at the back, and we had nothing but death to look forward to.

"We divided our food equally among us, and when it was done we expected to die, since no fruit or food of any kind was to be met with in that lonely place. "I spent my time wandering about the shore and lower part of the mountain, which I found to be very rich in precious stones; and amongst the wrecks that had been cast up on the shore I came across handsome goods and treasures of great value.

"I also noticed that a strange river of fresh water ran from the sea into a dark cave; and this I thought a great wonder, since in all other places rivers ran from the land into the sea, and not from the sea into the land.

"As our small stock of food got used up my companions grew weaker and weaker, and died one by one; and at last I, having been more careful than they in making my portion of food last out, was the only one left. I expected soon to follow my poor friends; but one day, just as I was coming to the end of my small store, I happened to wander near the bank of the great river that flowed from the sea into the cave which I had noticed before. As I gazed at this strange river I suddenly thought that it must have an outlet some-where, and, as I could not well be any worse off, I made up my mind to build a raft and allow the current to carry me where it would.

"Quick as thought I set to work, and soon built myself a strong raft with the pieces of wreckage that lay on the shore; then I loaded it with bales of rich stuffs, rubies, emeralds, and other precious stones I had found, together with the scrap of food I had left.

"When all was ready I took two little oars I had made and went on board; and having guided the raft carefully into the cave I allowed the strange river to carry me along.

"For several days I floated in utter darkness, and sometimes the roof of the cave was so low that it caught my head, and I had to lie flat upon the raft or I should have been killed.

"At last I came to the end of my food, and, being very weak and weary, I soon afterwards fell into a half-fainting state, and knew not what I did nor where I went.

"How long this dazed state lasted I don't know; but when I once more came to my senses and opened my eyes I found myself, to my great surprise, lying in a meadow on the bank of a river, where my raft was still floating, though it was now tied to a stake. A number of natives surrounded me; but though they spoke to me I could not understand what they said.

"Full of joy for my escape I uttered aloud a prayer of thankfulness in my own language; then one of the natives, who, it seemed, understood Arabic, came and spoke to me in the same tongue. He said that he and his companions belonged to the country I was in; and, having come to dig little canals from the strange river which flowed out of the great mountain close by, they had seen my raft and brought me off for safety to the shore.

"The natives gave me some food, and after refreshing myself I told them of all that had happened to me; and they thought my adventure so wonderful that they insisted I should go with them at once to their king and tell him my story.

"So I went with them to the capital of Serendib, as the island was called, and when we arrived at the royal palace they presented me to their king, who received me with such honour and kindness that I offered him the whole of the treasures upon my raft as a mark of my regard for him.

"But this truly noble prince refused to take any of my riches, and, instead, constantly added to them by handsome gifts of his own; and he was so struck with my wonderful adventures that he caused an account of them to be written in letters of gold and placed in his treasure-house.

"He gave orders for me to be treated with the same honour and respect as were his own great lords, and I was shown all the beauties and places of interest in the country, which I found to be very rich indeed in precious stones and rare plants.

"When I returned from viewing the country I begged the king to allow me to go back to my own land; and not only did he graciously consent, but also made me another splendid present of even greater value than any he had given me before. He also asked me to carry from him a letter to my sovereign lord, the Caliph Haroun Alraschid, together with a most noble gift. In the letter he humbly begged the caliph to accept his gift as a mark of the admiration and friendship he had for him; and the words were written in azure blue upon the skin of an animal of great value. The present consisted of spices and aloe wood; a cup, half a foot high, made out of a single ruby, and filled with enormous pearls; a snakeskin, the scales of which were said to possess certain healing powers; and lastly, a slave-maiden of dazzling beauty, whose robes were entirely covered with glittering jewels.

"I bade farewell to the king and his lords, and set sail in the fine ship that had been got ready for me, and as soon as I arrived in Bagdad I went to the royal palace and presented the caliph with the letter and the gift sent him by the King of Serendib.

"The caliph received his gift with much pleasure and great surprise at its richness, and he asked me if the King of Serendib was really so rich and splendid as one would suppose.

"I then gave him an account of the great magnificence of all I had seen in the island, telling him that the royal palace was covered with a hundred thousand rubies, that the king had in his treasure-house twenty thousand diamond crowns, and that when he went abroad he sat on a throne fixed on the back of an elephant, with a guard of a thousand men, clad in cloth of gold and silk, going before him, mounted on a hundred elephants all richly draped.

"The caliph was greatly interested to hear of this powerful king, whose riches were so wonderful, and when I had finished my story he sent me away with a handsome present."

Sindbad stopped here, and giving the porter his usual hundred sequins he invited him to come once again to hear the story of his last voyage. Hindbad and the other guests came next day at the proper time, and when dinner was over Sindbad began the story of his seventh and last voyage.

SINDBAD'S LAST VOYAGE

"I was glad to settle down in peace once more to enjoy my riches, and, since I was now getting on in years, I made up my mind to run no more risks of danger and adventures by land and sea, but to spend the rest of my days in ease and comfort.

"However, I had no sooner made up my mind to follow out this wise plan than one day the caliph sent for me to come before him at once. When I arrived at the palace the caliph told me that he wished to send a handsome gift to the King of Serendib, and he desired that I should be the bearer of it.

"I explained to the caliph that I had made up my mind to go to sea no more, and told him of the many terrible dangers I had gone through; but he still insisted that I should go, since it was most fitting that I, being already known to the king, should take the gift. He said that I only needed to take a letter and the gift to Serendib, and then return; so at last I agreed, and the caliph, well pleased, gave me a thousand sequins for my journey.

"After a few days I went on board ship, and set sail for Serendib, carrying with me the caliph's handsome gift and letter of friendly greeting. The gift consisted of many pieces of cloth of gold and of other rich stuffs; two splendid royal beds; a dish made of agate, an inch thick and half a foot wide; and a valuable tablet, said to have belonged to the great King Solomon.

"I arrived safely in Serendib, and going straight to the royal palace I presented to the king the letter and gift.

"The King of Serendib recognized me at once, and received me with much joy; and he was quite delighted with the friendly letter and the splendid present sent him by the caliph. He wished me to stay with him some time, but I begged to be excused, being anxious to return home; so he made me another gift, and allowed me to depart.

"I went on board and set sail, meaning to return to Bagdad at once; but, alas! this was not to be. A few days after we got out to sea we were attacked by fierce corsairs or sea-robbers, and in a very short time they captured our ship, and made prisoners of all on board. We were stripped of our clothes and made to put on ugly rags, and then the corsairs took us away to a strange country, and sold us as slaves.

"I was bought by a rich merchant, who took me to his house, dressed me in fine clothes, and treated me very kindly. Finding that I could shoot well with bow and arrow, he one day took me with him on an elephant to a thick forest some miles away from the town. Here we stopped, and putting a bow and arrows in my hand, he pointed to a tall tree, and said: 'Get up into that tree, and shoot at the elephants as they come past. There are a great number of them in this forest, and if you kill any of them, come and tell me.'

"He then gave me some food, and returned to the town, and I climbed up the tree and waited for the elephants to appear. None came near me that day, but early next morning a great herd of them came tramping past my tree. I shot my arrows into the midst of them, and at last I succeeded in killing the largest. I then returned to my master, who was very much pleased with what I had done; and after I had eaten some food, we went back to the forest and buried the dead elephant, my master meaning to return later to take its ivory tusks, which were of great value.

"After this I was sent every day into the forest to shoot elephants for my master; and then, one time, a very strange thing happened to me. It was about two months since I first became a slave, and I was sitting on my tree as usual, with my bow and arrows, when the herd of elephants, instead of passing by as they had always done before, came suddenly towards me with a great rush, making a dreadful noise. They quickly surrounded my tree, and stood staring solemnly at me for some time; then the largest of them suddenly put his trunk round my tree and, rooting it up, threw it to the ground. I fell off, but was not hurt; and then the elephant lift me up with his trunk, and setting me on his back, began to march forward at a great rate, followed by the whole herd.

"Presently he set me down on the ground again, and went away with his companions; and there I lay for some time, more dead than alive, as you may imagine.

"Finding that the elephants did not return, I got up and began to look about me. I found myself on a hillside which was almost covered with the bones and ivory tusks of elephants, and I soon made up my mind that this must be the burying-place of these strange creatures, which had evidently brought me there to show me that I should keep from harming them, since I only did so for the sake of their ivory tusks, to which I could now help myself without troubling them further.

"Quickly I left the hillside and returned to the city, which I reached in a day and a half, and when I told my master of my adventure, and of the vast treasures of ivory I had so unexpectedly come across, he was full of amazement. He showed great joy at seeing me again, for having found my uprooted tree, and bow and arrows, he had quite expected that I had been killed; and after I had rested and refreshed myself, we took an elephant and returned to the hillside of which I had told him. Here we loaded the elephant with as many fine ivory tusks as he could carry; and on our way back to the city my master said:

"Sindbad, I shall treat you no longer as a slave, for your discovery has made me rich for life. For years the forest elephants have killed great numbers of slaves; but you have been saved from their fury, which is a sign that Heaven favours you. All the merchants in the city will be grateful to you, for they will no longer need to risk the lives of their slaves, since there is ivory enough on that hillside to make all in our city rich and powerful. Not only do I make you free, but I will also give you great riches, and the next ship that comes into the harbour shall carry you back to your own land."

"I thanked my master for his kindness, and until a ship arrived I helped him to collect ivory. As soon as a vessel came into the harbour, it was got ready for me, being loaded with ivory and other valuable goods, as well as food for my voyage; and when all things were set in order I bade my late master farewell, and set sail. I traded on the voyage with my ivory, and bought splendid gifts for all my friends; and at last I arrived safely in Bagdad.

"I went at once to the caliph and told him of my adventures, which he thought so curious that he caused an account of them to be written in golden letters for himself.

"This was my last voyage, and at length I was able to settle down with my vast riches in peace and comfort."

When Sindbad finished his story, he said to Hindbad: "Now, my friend, you have heard what dangers I have gone through, and do you not think that after such troubles I deserve to live a life of peace and enjoyment?"

"Ah, yes, my lord," answered the porter, humbly kissing Sindbad's hand, "your sufferings and dangers have been terrible, and my own troubles and hardships are as nothing compared with yours. You are worthy of your riches, and I trust you will live long to enjoy them."

Sindbad was so pleased with this reply that he gave Hindbad yet another hundred sequins, and said he looked upon him as one of his best friends; and, begging of him to give up his work as a porter, he invited him to come and feast with him every day.

So Hindbad the porter became a rich and happy man, and all the rest of his life he had good cause to remember with a grateful mind the kindness of Sindbad the Sailor.

Codadad and his Brothers

Once upon a time there ruled in the city of Harran a very rich and powerful king, who was greatly beloved by his subjects because of his goodness and wisdom. This king would have been perfectly happy and contented had it not been for one thing—he had no children to reign after him. It made him sad to think that, when he died, his kingdom would pass into the hands of strangers, and he constantly prayed that Heaven would send him a child whom he could train up to rule the people as he himself had done.

At last his prayers were answered. One night, as he slept, there visited him in his dreams the dazzling figure of a prophet, who said to him: "You shall receive what you desire! Tomorrow morning, rise up early, say your prayers, and bow yourself twice to the ground. Then go into the palace garden and bid your gardener bring you a pomegranate. Eat as many of the seeds as you like, and then your wishes will certainly come to pass."

In the morning the king did as he was advised, and obtaining a ripe pomegranate, he counted out fifty seeds which he ate. Now at this time the king had fifty wives, and, to his great joy, before another year had gone by, a prince was born to each of these royal ladies.

It happened that one of the wives, a princess named

Pirouze, was on a visit to the king's cousin, Prince Samer of
Samaria, when her son was born. When the news was
brought to the King of Harran, although he was greatly
pleased, he desired his cousin to bring up Pirouze's child in
Samaria, since he himself now had so many children in his
palace. He told Prince Samer to give the royal baby the
name of Codadad, which means 'given of God', and not to
send him to Harran until he desired to receive him.

So Princess Pirouze and her son remained in the palace of
the Prince of Samaria, who brought up the young prince in a
fitting manner, and provided him with suitable masters,
who taught him everything that it was proper for one of his
high rank to know.

Codadad grew up handsome, clever, and amiable, and at
eighteen years of age it would not have been possible to
find anywhere a more accomplished and charming young
prince.

Now Codadad, although he had received every kindness
and care from the Prince of Samaria, did not feel satisfied at
being kept away from his father and brothers, and one day
he said to his mother: "Dear madam, I am tired of living
here in Samaria at my ease. I long to gain glory in warfare
and adventures, and I beg of you to allow me to leave you
and go out into the world to seek for fame! Why does not
my father, the King of Harran, send for me to help him to
fight against the many enemies I know he has? It is not right
that my brothers should have this honour alone, and I cannot bear to wait here any longer. Since he does not send for
me, I shall go to my father as a stranger, and offer to fight
for him, and I shall not let him know who I am until I have
done some glorious deed. Then, when he knows that I am
his own son, he will be proud of me, and in this way he will
have learnt to love and admire me for my own worth, and
not for my princely rank."

Pirouze, seeing that her son had such a noble purpose in
view, was ready to approve of his plan; and one morning
Codadad bade her farewell, and left the palace as though he

meant to go hunting, without saying anything about the matter to the Prince of Samaria, who might have refused to let him go.

The young prince looked very brave and noble as he rode along on a white horse shod with gold and draped with blue satin sewn with pearls. He was very handsomely dressed, and carried a bow and arrows slung over his shoulders, whilst at his side hung a sword set with dazzling jewels, the hilt of which was formed of a single diamond, which flashed like lightning in the sunshine.

When he arrived in Harran he went at once to the palace to offer his services as a soldier to the king, declaring that he was the son of a nobleman of Grand Cairo, and that be had left his own country to travel and seek for adventures and glory in warfare. And the King of Harran was so delighted with his fine looks and manly bearing that he at once made him an important officer in his army.

Codadad soon gained great fame in the army for his bravery and skill, and was admired by all the officers and soldiers. By his noble conduct and the charm of his manners he soon became the chief favourite of the king, who grew to love him so much that he was never satisfied unless the handsome young stranger was by his side.

The only persons who refused to admire Codadad were the forty-nine young princes, his brothers, who grew so jealous of him on account of the favour he had gained with the king, that they looked upon the young stranger with bitter hatred, little guessing that he was

their own brother. And when at last the king, to show his trust in the new favourite, made Codadad the adviser and governor of the young princes, and put them under his charge, their jealousy knew no bounds, and, full of spiteful rage, they made up their minds to get rid of the "upstart stranger" as they called him. They would quickly have found some means of killing him outright, but feared, by so doing, that they would bring upon themselves the anger of the king, who loved his new favourite so dearly that he would certainly punish anyone who harmed him; so they decided that their safest plan would be to try and bring Codadad into disgrace with their father, who would then banish him from court.

At last they thought of a scheme. They arranged to ask Codadad to give them leave to go hunting by themselves at some distance, meaning to ride away and hide in some other city for awhile. They hoped that their father, thinking them to be lost, would blame Codadad for neglecting to attend them himself, and probably order him to be put to death for such careless conduct.

Having arranged this spiteful plan, the young princes went one day to Codadad and asked him to allow them to go hunting by themselves, promising that they would return early in the evening; and Codadad, thinking this request harmless enough, willingly granted them leave to do so.

The young princes set off, but did not return; and when they had been gone for three days, the king sent for Codadad to know what had become of his sons. Codadad respectfully explained the matter to the king, and tried to satisfy him that there was no cause for alarm; but when another day passed by and still the young princes did not return, the King of Harran flew into a great passion, and cried out angrily to Codadad: "Careless stranger, you have not done your duty ! Why did you allow my sons to go out of your sight? Go and look for them at once, and unless you bring them back to me I will have you put to death!"

Codadad, full of alarm, and grieved at having brought such trouble upon his father, to whom he had hoped to be a help and comfort, left the palace at once, and mounting his horse he set off to look for the young princes, searching all over the country and asking at every village if they had passed that way.

After vainly searching for some days he at length came to a great plain, in the midst of which he could see a huge palace built entirely of black marble. He rode up to this castle, and at one of the open barred windows he saw a beautiful lady, whose clothes were in rags and whose long hair was in disorder. She called out to him wildly: "Turn back at once, young stranger! A terrible black giant lives here, who feeds upon human beings, and he will certainly destroy you, for he seizes all who come this way, shutting them up in dark dungeons until he is ready to eat them!"

"But, lady," said Codadad, "I cannot go and leave you here to die! Who are you, and how came you to such a sad pass?"

"I am a lady of Grand Cairo," answered the poor prisoner. "I and my servants were riding past this castle yesterday, when we met this dreadful black giant, who killed all my attendants and brought me here, where I know that only death awaits me! But you may yet escape, and I beg of you to fly before the black returns from chasing some travellers whom he saw a short time since on the plain!"

But even as the lady spoke the black came into sight, riding on a huge dusky horse. He was a hideous giant, and carried a great sword in his hand; but, though Codadad was astonished at his enormous size, he did not lose courage, and drawing his own trusty weapon he stood and waited for his enemy.

As soon as the monster drew near, Codadad rushed at him at once, and wounded him on the knee. The giant, uttering a horrible yell of rage, raised his great sword, meaning to cut the young man in half. But Codadad sprang skilfully out of the way, and before the black could raise his sword again he struck him such a heavy blow on his right arm that he cut it off.

The giant fell to the ground with a crash, and Codadad, rushing up to him at once, cut off his head before he could recover himself.

The beautiful lady uttered a cry of joy from the window, and called out to Codadad to search the giant's pockets for the keys of the castle, that he might set her free.

Codadad did so; and having taken the keys from the giant's pocket, he opened the gates of the castle, and entered. The lady came rushing to meet him at once, falling on her knees to thank him for having saved her, and praising him as the greatest hero in the world; and Codadad was so delighted with her dazzling beauty and grateful words that he fell in love with her immediately.

Whilst they were talking they heard the sound of groans and wailing voices, which the lady said belonged to the other victims of the giant, and who, awaiting death, were bemoaning their sad fate in the dungeons of the castle. Codadad at once took the keys and set them free. He told the poor prisoners that he had killed the giant, and that their lives were safe; and amidst loud cries of joy, he and the beautiful lady unbound them from the stakes to which they had been tied.

There were about a hundred of these poor captives, and to the great surprise and delight of Codadad he found amongst them the young princes, whom he had come to seek. He respectfully embraced them with much joy, saying how anxious the King had been on their account, and how glad he was to have found them again. Then, turning to the other captives whom he had set free, and who were chiefly merchants, he told them to seek out their goods from amongst the treasures that lay on every side, and then return to their homes.

Each merchant found his own goods, and Codadad divided the rest of the treasures equally amongst them. The merchants also found that their camels and horses were still safe in the stables, and having first thanked the young prince many times for having saved their lives, mounted and rode away.

When the merchants had gone, Codadad turned to the beautiful lady, and asked her where she wished to go, declaring that he and the King of Harran's sons would not leave her until they had taken her back safely to her friends in her own country.

"I have left my own country for ever," the lady said to Codadad; "and since you have saved my life, I think I ought to tell you my story, for I am not a lady of Cairo, as I first led you to suppose. I am a princess. My father was lately killed by one who seized the throne for himself, and I have had to fly in order to save my own life!"

Codadad and the young princess, full of pity and interest, begged that the princess would tell them her story, promising to help her in every way; and after thanking them for their kindness, she began:

"My father was the king of the great island city of Deryabar; and I am his only child. Although he would rather have been blessed with a son, he did not love meany the less and he caused me to be taught and brought up with every care, that I might be able to rule the kingdom after his death.

"It happened one day that my father went hunting, and was so eager in the chase of a wild ass that he rode on till night, having left his attendants far behind; and entering a wood as darkness came on, he made his way towards a light he could see not far ahead. He found that the light came from the fire of a hut, through the open window of which he saw, to his horror, a black giant, who was roasting an ox before the fire. In a far corner of the hut there crouched a beautiful lady, who seemed full of grief and terror. Her hands were bound together; and beside her there lay a child of about two or three years of age who joined his cries and tears to those of his mother.

"My father, though full of pity for the poor lady and her child, felt it would be useless for him to enter the hut just then, since the giant would quickly overcome him; so he waited outside, and watched for a chance of being able to help her. Presently the giant began to talk to the lady, saying that if she would try to love him he would treat her with more kindness and respect; but the lady declared that he was an evil monster, whom she would never cease to regard with horror. This put the giant into a fearful rage; and, seizing the poor lady by her long hair, he was just about to cut her head off with his sword, when my father, who had waited for this opportunity, drew his bow, and sent an arrow right through his heart. The giant fell dead upon the floor; and my father entered the hut, and, unbinding the lady's hands, asked who she was, and whence she came. The lady replied that she was the wife of a Saracen prince, and had been stolen away from her home by this black giant, who had been one of her husband's chief attendants, and who had fallen in love with her. She declared that the monster had carried her so far away from her own country that she knew not how to return; and as my father felt great pity for her, he took her back with him to his palace, together with her little son, trusting that her husband would come to claim her sooner or later. The Saracen lady was very glad to find a place of safety; but though my father did all he could in the matter, he could not get any news of her friends, and her husband never came to claim her. As he would not now turn her adrift, he allowed her to remain in his palace with her child, whom he caused to be brought up and taught in a fitting manner.

"The Saracen lady's son grew up to be a handsome young man, but the favours which my father showed him, and the praises of the lords and the ladies of the court, made him so vain and conceited that he took it for granted that he would certainly receive me as his bride, and become the next ruler in Deryabar. And when my father did not show any haste in this matter, he even went so far as to demand me of him in a very haughty manner.

"My father said that he had plans for a more important marriage for me; and the ungrateful young man, forgetting the kindness he had always received, was so enraged at this reply that he found means to kill my father, and make himself king in his place. No sooner had he done this wicked deed than he sent for me, meaning either to force me to marry him or else put me to death; but, happily, my father's grand vizier managed to hurry me away from the palace with one of my ladies before the messenger arrived. We got on board a vessel, the grand vizier intending to take me for safety to the palace of some neighbouring king; but before we had been at sea more than a few days, a dreadful storm arose, and our ship was dashed to pieces against a rock.

"The grand vizier, my lady attendant, and all the others on board were drowned before my eyes; but I managed to cling to a piece of the wreck, and was cast senseless upon a coast which I had never seen before. I had scarcely opened my eyes when a number of gay horsemen appeared upon the shore, who, I soon learnt, were the king of that country and his lords. Surprised to see a strange lady in such a wretched state upon the shore, one of the attendants led me up to the king, who was a young man of very great beauty. I told him my story; and the young king felt such pity for me that he took me to his palace, and desired his mother to allow me to live with her. The queen treated me with great kindness, so that I became happy once more; and when the handsome young king fell in love with me, and wished me to marry him, I was very willing to do so.

"Soon afterwards such a host of enemies came swarming into the land, that we were overpowered; and the king and I were only just able to escape before the palace was taken. We managed to get into a little fishing-boat, and in this were tossed about by the waves until we came up with a large vessel. Thinking this was a merchant ship, we hailed it; and then, to our horror, we found that the men on board, instead of being merchants, were pirates. The pirates seized our boat, and, binding our hands, dragged us on board; and when they saw that I was fair to look upon, they began to quarrel amongst themselves as to who should have me. They soon came to blows, and fought so fiercely that at last all lay dead but one, who claimed me as his own, declaring that he would give me to a friend of his, to whom he had promised a beautiful slave.

"The pirate then seized the poor prince, my husband, and threw him into the waves; and, seeing that I was about to cast myself in after him, he bound me close with cords to the mast of the ship, where he left me to shriek and weep at my sad fate. When we came to land, the pirate took me on shore, where he obtained camels, and carried me, along with other slaves he had bought, in the direction of Cairo, meaning to present me to the friend he had mentioned. However, we had not been many days upon the road when we fell in with the terrible black giant who has just met with the reward he deserved. He soon killed the pirate and his followers, and brought me to this dreadful castle, where I had nothing to which to look forward but horror and death.

"The remainder of my story you know; and as for my future, that rests with you, for I know not where to go, nor what to do!"

When the Princess of Deryabar had finished the story of her adventures, Codadad felt so much pity for her sad and lonely state, and such admiration for her beauty and charming manners, that he said:

"Dear lady, let me beg of you to forget your past troubles, for it is in your power to be happy in the future. I feel sure that the father of these princes, the good King of Harran, will gladly receive you at his court. If you will accept of my love and protection, it will be the greatest happiness of my life to marry you now, in the presence of these princes!"

The princess, who had from the first been charmed with the handsome looks and noble conduct of Codadad, consented very readily, and the wedding took place that day in the giant's castle, where plenty of food was found to provide a suitable feast. After the marriage-feast was over, they all mounted their horses and set off for the King of Harran's palace, taking wine and food with them and all things necessary for the journey.

One evening, after they had travelled several days, Codadad discovered himself to his brothers. He told them who he really was, how he had been brought up in Samaria, and why he had come as a stranger to his father's court; and he begged the princes to receive him as their brother, which they did.

But although the young princes pretended to receive their brother kindly, they were, in reality, more madly jealous of him than ever, knowing that their father would now certainly prefer him to themselves, because of the splendid deed he had just done; and instead of feeling grateful to him for having saved their lives, they were filled with envy and anger, and agreed amongst themselves to kill him. They laid their plans quickly; and that very night, as Codadad lay sleeping in his tent, they rushed upon him, and, stabbing him many times, left him for dead in the arms of the shrieking Princess of Deryabar.

They then went on with their journey, and next day arrived at the palace of the King of Harran.

When they were asked by their father where they had been, they did not mention anything about the black giant or about Codadad, but only said that they had been visiting some of the neighbouring cities, which they had long been curious to see.

In the meanwhile the poor Princess of Deryabar was left weeping beside the still form of her husband, whom at first she thought was dead; but presently noticing that he still breathed, she ran out of the tent, and made her way to the nearest town to seek for a surgeon. She soon found one, who returned with her at once; but when they arrrived at the tent, they found that Codadad had disappeared!

Feeling sure that some wild beast had entered and dragged him away to his lair, the princess renewed her tears and cries of woe; and the surgeon felt such pity for her he persuaded her to return with him to his house in the town, where he promised to do everything he could to help her.

So the unhappy princess returned with her new friend to his house, and after she had rested and refreshed herself the surgeon begged of her to tell him the whole story of her adventures. The princess did so; and when she had finished, the surgeon said:

"You must not give way to grief, my dear lady, for it is certainly your duty to avenge your husband's wrongs. Let me beg of you to go to the King of Harran, and tell him how cruelly Prince Codadad has been treated by his jealous brothers. I am sure he will do you justice; and I will gladly go with you as your protector!"

The princess thanked the surgeon for his kindness, and said, if he would accompany her, she would do as he advised her; and next day, mounted on camels, they set out for the city of Harran.

When they arrived in Harran they went to an inn, where they asked for news of the court. They were told that the king was in great trouble, since he had lost one of his sons, a prince named Codadad, whose mother, the Princess Pirouzé, had just arrived in the city with the news that his son had left the court of Samaria, where he had been brought up, and had not been heard of since, although she had caused constant searches to be made for him.

On hearing this, the surgeon thought it would be well for them to see the Princess Pirouzé first, before visiting the King of Harran; and since it was not safe for the Princess of Deryabar to run the risk of being seen by the king's sons, he made up his mind to go out alone, and to find a means of bringing his charge safely into the presence of her husband's mother.

So he left the princess to rest at the inn, and went out by himself, walking towards the palace. But before he got there he met a party of ladies on mules, attended by guards and black slaves. Seeing that the chief of these ladies was very richly dressed, and appeared to be of importance, he asked a bystander who she was. He was told that the lady was one of the king's chief wives, the Princess Pirouzé, who was on her way to the mosque to pray for the return of her lost son, Prince Codadad.

The surgeon was glad to have so soon come across the very person whom he was seeking; but as the crowd prevented him from getting near to Pirouzé, he took aside one of her slaves and whispered to him that he had news for the princess of her lost son. The slave told him to follow the procession on its return to the palace, and he would then find means to bring him before his mistress.

The surgeon did so, and on arriving at the palace he was
met by the same slave, who said that the Princess Pirouzé
was full of eagerness to hear the news he had brought. He
was taken at once into the room where Pirouzé sat with her
attendants, and after he had bowed low before her, the princess desired him to tell her what news he had brought of her
son. He then described to her all that the Princess of
Deryabar had told him of what had taken place between
Codadad and his brothers; and when he spoke of how cruelly the poor young prince had been stabbed, the grief-
stricken mother fainted away. When she had been restored
to herself by her ladies the surgeon went on to tell her of his
meeting with the Princess of Deryabar, and of the disappearance of Codadad; and when he had finished, Pirouzé
said: "Your services and kindness shall be well rewarded.
Go back now to the Princess of Deryabar and tell her that
the King of Harran will soon receive her as his son's wife!"

The surgeon left the room, and when he had gone,
Pirouzé gave full vent to her tears, for she felt now that her
son was indeed lost to her for ever. She was still weeping
when the King of Harran entered the room; and upon his
asking if she had heard worse news of her lost son, she told
him the whole story she had just heard from the surgeon.

When the king heard of the wicked conduct of the young
princes, he was full of anger and declared that they would
quickly receive the punishment of death, which they deserved. He ordered his grand vizier to a large number of
richly-dressed lords and attendants with him; and presently
he returned with the princess, mounted on a beautiful white
mule decked with gold and jewels. She was attended by the
surgeon, who was also mounted on a handsome horse,
which had been sent to him as a present from the king; and
crowds of people stood in the streets to welcome the strange
princess as she passed by.

When the Princess of Deryabar arrived at the palace she
was received with every mark of respect and kindness by
the King of Harran, who at once took her into the presence

of the Princess Pirouzé, who embraced her many times.

The two princesses and the king were quite overcome by the sadness of their meeting, and wept together for some time; and the Princess of Deryabar repeated her story, and begged the king to avenge the cruel treatment of her husband, Prince Codadad.

The king replied that the ungrateful young princes should certainly die; but he first of all gave orders that the people should be told of the death of Codadad, that they might know he was acting justly. He also caused a great tomb of white marble to be set up in a pleasant plain close by; and when it was ready he went with his whole court to take part in a great funeral service held in honour of his dead son.

When this service was over, the king ordered public prayers to be said in all the mosques for eight days; and on the ninth day he arranged that the young princes, his son, to be beheaded.

However, the execution had to be delayed, for news was suddenly brought that a great host of wild enemies were marching towards the city to make war upon the King of Harran. All the people were in terror, and wept again for the loss of the brave Codadad, who, they felt, would have been of such help to them in this time of need; but the King of Harran quickly gathered together as large an army as he could, and went bravely forward to meet his foes just outside the city, where a great battle was fought.

Now, although the King of Harran and his men fought very bravely indeed, they could not drive back their enemies, whose numbers were far greater than their own; but just as they were about to be overcome, a very strange thing happened. A large body of splendid horsemen suddenly appeared, and rushed upon the King of Harran's enemies with such force that they turned and fled away in dismay, followed by the strangers, who overtook and killed the greater number of them.

The King of Harran was overjoyed at this sudden turn of affairs, and felt very grateful to the strange horsemen who had come to his help; and when the battle was won, he rode up to thank their leader, whom he had admired for the wonderful bravery he had shown. He was eager to learn the name of this hero; but great was his astonishment on drawing nearer to recognize in the brave stranger his own lost son, Codadad!

"Your Majesty is doubtless surprised to see one whom you must have thought to be dead ! "said the young prince. "But, happily, Heaven has saved me to help you against your enemies!"

"My dear son, what a joyful meeting is this!" cried the king, throwing himself into the arms of Codadad, and embracing him many times. He then told Codadad that he knew the story of his adventures with the black giant, and of the cruel treatment which he had received at the hands of his brothers; and when the astonished young prince asked how he could possibly have learnt of these things, the king explained to him how the Princess of Deryabar had been brought to Harran by the good surgeon, and was even now in the palace together with his mother, the Princess Pirouzé.

Codadad was delighted to know that his wife and mother were both so close at hand; and since there was now no further need to remain on the field of battle, he returned with his father to the palace. Great crowds of people followed them, uttering cries of joy and shouting out their praises of the brave Codadad who had driven away their enemies.

Directly they arrived at the palace, the King of Harran led Codabad into the room where his mother, Pirouzé, and his wife, the Princess of Deryabar, were sitting, and you can imagine the joyful meeting that took place! When they had all rejoiced together, and embraced each other tenderly many times, the king begged Codadad to tell them the story of his escape from death.

The young prince replied that after the Princess of Deryabar had left him to go in search of a surgeon, a peasant had come into the tent quite by accident, and seeing him lying wounded and senseless upon the ground, had lifted him up, and, placing him upon a mule which he had outide, had taken him to his own hut, where he had tended his wounds with such skill and care that they had healed in a wonderfully short time.

As soon as he felt better he had given the peasant all the jewels be had about his clothing, and, gratefully thanking him for the care hc had taken of him, started for the palace at Harran. But hearing on his way that a host of enemies were about to attack his father's city, he had stirred up the people in the villages round about, and persuaded them to join him in coming to the aid of their master, the King of Harran. He had soon gathered a strong band of brave young men together, and, as we have seen, just arrived in time to win a victory for his father, and drive the enemy away.

When Codadad had finished his story, and also listened to the adventures of the Princess of Deryabar, the King of Harran declared that the execution of the young princes, his sons, would be delayed no longer; but Codadad begged so hard that his brothers might be pardoned and allowed to live, that at length his father consented.

So the young princes were brought from their prison, and Codadad himself took off their chains, and, embracing them each in turn, said he gladly forgave them for their unkindness, and begged that they would now learn to love him.

Thc good surgeon was next sent for to receive the thanks of Codadad for the kindness he had shown to his wife, and when he left the palace he was loaded with gold and other valuable gifts.

Rejoicings and thanksgivings for the great victory that had been gained were held all over the city of Harran for many weeks, and when they were over, Prince Codadad settled down with his beautiful wife, the Princess of Deryabar, to a long life of perfect peace and happiness.

Ali Baba
and the Forty Thieves

Once upon a time there lived in a certain town of Persia two brothers, whose names were Ali Baba and Cassim. These two, although they were brothers, were not alike in any way, nor were they on the best of terms. Now Cassim was rich, and Ali Baba was very poor. What little means their father had was divided equally between them at his death; but Cassim, by marrying a rich wife, became a great merchant, and was able to live in much comfort. Ali Baba's wife, though she loved him well, brought him no riches at all, and was as badly off as himself. So he still remained a poor man, gaining a wretched living by cutting wood in a forest near by, and carrying it about the town to sell on three asses, which made up the whole of his wealth.

Although Ali Baba was so poor, he was of a much better and kinder disposition than his more fortunate brother; for Cassim was haughty, unloving, and grasping, and at last his great greediness brought sad trouble upon him, as you will see.

One day, Ali Baba went out into the forest as usual, to cut wood, taking with him his three asses to carry home the results of his hard work. He had just finished his humble task, having cut as much wood as his asses could carry, when suddenly he noticed in the distance a great cloud of dust, which seemed to be moving towards him. He looked at it very carefully, and soon saw that it was caused by a body of men galloping swiftly along on horseback.

Now, Ali Baba was by no means a dull man, for he had his wits about him; and thinking that these strange horsemen might perhaps prove to be fierce robbers, he quickly made up his mind to keep out of their way. Seeing a large tree growing beside a steep, craggy rock close at hand, he climbed up into the midst of it, so that though he was completely hidden from sight, yet he could see what the horsemen were doing down below.

The party came forward at a great rate, and to the surprise and dismay of Ali Baba they drew in close to his hiding-place. The poor wood-cutter took a good look at the men as they dismounted and tied their horses to the trees and shrubs around. Judging from their wild, fierce looks, and the heavy bags which they carried, he felt quite sure that they must be robbers. Nor, indeed, was he wrong in his guess, for they were none other than a band of robbers who carried on their plundering some distance away and had their meeting place at that spot.

He counted forty of them altogether, and noticed that one, who had the finest appearance, seemed to be their captain or leader, since he gave orders, which the others obeyed. When they had all tied up their horses, this man came forward, and, standing in front of the great rock beside which Ali Baba's tree stood, he called out these words: *"Open, Sesame!"*

Ali Baba bent forward with breathless eagerness, and to his great astonishment, as soon as the robber captain spoke these words, a door flew open in the rock. Then the forty men, carrying their heavy bags on their shoulders, all marched through the opening, and then the door shut of its own accord.

Ali Baba did not dare to stir from his hiding-place for fear the robbers should suddenly come out and see him, so he waited patiently where he was for some time, until at last the door in the rock flew open once more.

The robbers all trooped out, with empty bags this time,

and quickly mounted their horses; and their captain, after saying *"Shut, Sesame!"* upon which the door closed, placed himself at the head of them, and they all rode off.

Having waited until the robbers were quite a long way off, Ali Baba came down from his tree; and then, being very curious to know what was to be seen on the other side of the door in the rock, he made up his mind to try to enter. He remembered the words that the robber captain had used; so, making his way through the bushes, he stood before the rock, and cried: *"Open, Sesame!"* The door flew open at once; and as soon as the wood-cutter entered, it shut of its own accord.

Ali Baba was surprised to find himself in a large cave well lighted from an opening at the top, and full of wonderful treasures on every side. There were bales of silk and rich cloths, handsome carpets piled one above another, great heaps of solid gold and silver, in heavy bars; to say nothing of fat bulging bags full of money and priceless jewels, which filled every odd space.

The poor wood-cutter at once guessed that this cave had been the home and storehouse of robbers for a great many years; and since the treasures had already been stolen in the first place, probably years ago, he did not think it wrong to help himself now. So he quickly gathered together as many of the bags of gold as he thought his three asses could carry, and got them safely outside; being careful to say the words *"Shut, Sesame!"* when he came out for the last time, so that the robbers would find the door in the rock closed when they came again, and would not know that their hiding-place was discovered.

Then he found his asses, which had strayed to some little distance, and loaded them with the bags of gold, over which he carefully piled wood, so that they were hidden; and when all was ready he went back to town.

When he got to the wretched hut that was his home, he took the bags inside, and poured out the gold in a great shining heap upon the floor.

His poor wife was full of surprise and delight at this beautiful sight. She listened in amazement to the wonderful tale that Ali Baba had to tell, and, when he had finished, she was eager to count the money. But Ali Baba said this would take too long a time, for he wanted to bury the money in the garden at once, thinking it better to keep his new riches a secret at present, since he did not wish others to know of the treasure-house he had found.

However, his wife said that she would at least weigh the gold, whilst he was digging the hole for it; and since she had not a measure of her own large enough, she went to the house of Cassim, her brother-in-law, to borrow one.

Now, Cassim's wife was curious to know what Ali Baba and his wife could want to measure in such a hurry, seeing that they were so very poor; so she took the trouble to smear the bottom of the measure with fat, which would tell her what kind of corn had been weighed in it, since some of the grains would most likely get buried in the fat.

Ali Baba's wife quickly took the measure to her own house, and, not noticing the fat at the bottom, carefully weighed the gold. She then took the measure back, and her husband buried his treasure.

As soon as Cassim's wife was alone she looked at the measure, and noticed a small piece of gold that had stuck to the fat at the bottom. She was filled with envy at the thought that Ali Baba, whom she had always understood to be so poor, had so much gold as to need to measure it.

When her husband came home she showed him the piece of money she had found in the measure; and Cassim, instead of being pleased that his brother at one time very poor was now evidently rich, became so full of rage and jealousy that he could not sleep all night.

Directly morning came he went to Ali Baba to demand how it came about that he had so much money as to need to weigh it; and he showed him the piece of gold found in the measure.

Ali Baba saw that he could not keep his secret from his brother, and so he told Cassim all about the robber's cave, and of his adventure on the day before.

Now, Cassim was a very greedy man indeed, and, although he was already quite rich enough, he wanted to be still richer; so, as he had never behaved kindly to his brother, he now very haughtily ordered Ali Baba to tell him exactly where the robber's cave was to be found, or he would tell the rulers of the town that his brother was a thief, and so get him into trouble.

Ali Baba was thus obliged to tell his unkind brother all he wished, even to the very words that would open the door in the rock; and then greedy Cassim went away, making up his mind to visit the cave at once and take away all the treasures for himself, so that his brother could get no more.

So early next morning, before anyone else was awake, he set off with ten mules loaded with empty chests to hold the treasure, and quickly made his way along the paths that Ali Baba had told him to take. In this manner he soon found the rock, and standing before it, he uttered the magic words: *"Open, Sesame!"*

The door flew open as he had been told it would, and when he stepped inside the cave it closed again. Cassim was full of astonishment and delight, for even his greedy mind had never dreamed of such wonderful riches as he saw on every side of him.

He soon set to work to drag as many of the bags of gold as he could lift towards the door; but his thoughts were so full of his new riches, and of the fine figure he would cut with them, that when he was ready to go he could not think of the magic word that would open the door for him.

Now, sesame is a certain kind of grain, and Cassim knew that the word he had forgotten was the name of corn of some kind; but, try as he would, he could not remember the exact word. He said: *"Open, Sesame!"*, and cried out the name of every other kind of grain he could remember; but none of these was the right word, and so the door remained shut.

The more he tried to remember the word, the more confused he got; and at last he threw down the money-bags he held in his hands, and rushed about the cave in despair, trying to find another way out. But all his efforts were in vain; and when, at noon, he heard the noise of galloping horses, which told him the robbers were returning, he was full of fear, and felt that his last hour had come.

However, Cassim made up his mind to try and escape so when at length the door flew open at the magic word *"Sesame"*, which he had not been able to remember, he rushed out and tried to get away. But the robbers saw him at once, and seizing the wretched man, they soon killed him with their sabres.

The robbers were much alarmed to find that their hiding-place had been discovered, and they could not imagine how Cassim could have got into the cave, since they had always thought that no one but themselves knew of the magic phrase which would open the door. Fearing lest the man whom they had just killed might have shared the secret with others, they cut his dead body into four pieces, hanging two quarters on either side of the cave door, to frighten anyone else who might be so bold as to enter. When they had done this, they once more mounted their horses and rode away to rob all whom they met.

When Cassim's wife found that her husband did not return home at nightfall, she was afraid that something dreadful must have happened to him; and early next morning she went to Ali Baba to tell him of her fears. Ali Baba did what he could to comfort her; and then, forgetting all about his brother's greediness and unkind behaviour to himself, he at once set off, with his three asses, to find out what had become of him.

When he came to the robbers' hiding-place, he stood beside the rock and called out: *"Open, Sesame!"* and the door flew open as before. The first sight that met his eyes was Cassim's divided body; and full of horror at his brother's sad end, he took down the four pieces, and wrapping them up, he placed them on one of his asses to take home with him. Then he loaded the other two asses with bags of gold, covering them over with wood as before; and when he had again named the magic word that closed the door of the cave, he started off home once more, being careful to wait at the end of the forest until night had set in, that he might pass through the town in the dark.

Having put his new treasures in safety, he went on to his sister-in-law's house, taking Cassim's dead body with him. The door was opened by a clever and beautiful young slave girl, named Morgiana, whom Ali Baba well knew could be trusted with a secret; so he told her of what had happened to her master, saying that the manner of his death must be kept a secret, and that his friends must be told that he had died in a natural way. Morgiana promised to do all she could to carry out this plan; and then she went to call her mistress.

When Cassim's wife saw her husband's dead body, and heard how he had met with his death, she was in great grief; but Ali Baba soon thought of a way to comfort her. He said that he himself was ready to marry her, and share his new riches with her, if she would keep the secret of the robbers' cave, and let her friends think that Cassim had died a natural death. Since it was a custom of the country for a man to marry his brother's widow, and take her to live with his own wife, there was nothing strange in the offer.

So Cassim's widow, feeling lonely, and knowing that her brother-in-law was now a very rich man, was quite willing to become his wife; and being greatly comforted by the thought that she would still be cared for, she agreed to all the plans of Ali Baba, and promised to keep the true manner of Cassim's death a secret.

Now, Morgiana was really a very clever girl indeed, and she soon thought of a fine plan to help her mistress in this matter. As soon as Ali Baba had returned to his own home, she went out to a shop where medicines were sold, and asked for some special lozenges very good in case of bad illness. When the man in the shop asked who was ill at Cassim's house she told him that it was her master himself, and that he was in a very bad state indeed. Next morning she went again to the same shop, and bought a certain medicine only given to sick persons likely to die, saying she feared her master would not get better now. As Ali Baba and his wife also went many times backwards and forwards with sad faces between the two houses, no one was surprised, when evening came, to learn that Cassim was dead; and all were ready to believe that he had died in the ordinary way.

The next thing to be done was to dispose of the dead body, so that no one should find out that it had been cut into four pieces; but Morgiana was not at a loss. Early next morning she went to the stall of an old cobbler, named Baba Mustapha, who she knew would be at work before anyone else was up; and putting a piece of gold into his hand, she asked him to take his needle and thread and go with her to do some important work, saying, however, that she must blindfold him at the end of the street, for she did not wish him to know where she was taking him.

Baba Mustapha at first did not like the idea of such a strange errand; but he was a merry, obliging old fellow, and when Morgiana put another piece of gold in his hand and promised him a third piece when his task was done, he agreed to go with her. They set off at once, and at the end of the street Morgiana tied a handkerchief over the old cobbler's eyes, and did not take it off until she had brought him into the very room where her dead master's quartered body lay.

Then she told him to take his needle and thread, and carefully sew the pieces together; and when he had finished, she gave him a third piece of gold, and, blindfolding him again, she led him back to his own street, going in a very roundabout way, up and down many streets, in order to confuse him, and feeling satisfied that he could not know where he had been.

Now that Cassim's body had been put together again, it was buried in the usual way, without anyone discovering the secret of his death. A few days later, Ali Baba took his wife and belongings, and went to live in his brother's house; and a short time after he married Cassim's widow, as he had promised, and began to enjoy his new-found riches.

In the meantime, the forty thieves were beginning to feel very uneasy. When they next came back to their cave, and saw that Cassim's dead body had been taken away, together with some of their treasure-bags, they knew for certain that someone else knew of their hiding-place; and the captain, fearing that they were in danger of being captured, suggested that one of the band should go disguised into the town at the end of the forest, and try to find out all he could from the people's talk about the man they had killed, since it was evident his friends would know of the manner in which he had met his death.

One of the robbers willingly offered to do as the captain asked, even when he was told that if he gave their secret to anyone, or failed in his task, he would be killed; and after dressing himself in such a way that no one could guess that he was a fierce robber, he said good-bye to his companions and set out, entering the town just at daybreak.

No one was about so early in the day; but, as it happened, the spy walked past the stall of the cobbler, Baba Mustapha, who was always up betimes, and seeing the old fellow already at work, he bid him good-day, saying that he must have good eyesight if he could see to work when the daylight was still so faint.

The old cobbler replied that his eyes were indeed very good, for it was not long ago that he had managed to sew up a dead body in a room where there was even less light than he had at present.

When the robber heard this, he was full of joy, for he felt sure he had got on the right track straightaway; but he pretended to be much surprised, and putting a piece of gold into the old cobbler's hand, he asked him to point out the house where he had done such a strange piece of work.

Baba Mustapha said he could not do this, since he had been led blindfold to the house, and did not know what streets he had passed through; but when the robber put another piece of gold into his hand, and suggested that perhaps if he were blindfolded again he might remember the turnings he had taken, the cobbler said he would try.

So, at the end of the street, the old cobbler allowed himself to be blindfolded by the robber, and then taking his hand, he led him through several streets he now remembered to have passed along, until at last he stopped in front of Cassim's house, saying this was as far as he had been taken before.

The robber took a piece of chalk out of his pocket and carefully marked the door of the house, that he might know it again; and then, taking the bandage off the cobbler's eyes, he thanked him for his trouble, and told him to return to his stall. When old Baba Mustapha had trotted off, the robber went back to the forest to tell his companions what he had found out and done, feeling sure that they would be pleased with him. But his morning's work was soon spoilt for him, as you will see.

He had not been long gone out of the street when Morgiana happened to come out of the house, and her quick eyes at once noticed the strange chalk mark on her master's door. After looking at it for some time, and thinking that it might mean danger to Ali Baba, she felt she must guard against it; so, fetching a piece of chalk, she carefully marked several other doors on each side, in exactly the same way, that her master's house might not be known by this sign.

In the meantime, the robber had returned to the cave, and told his news; and when his story was done the captain said that they must now go into the town and do away with their enemy as soon as possible. Since forty men entering the town at once would cause surprise, the robbers decided to go in parties of two or three, and all meet together in a great square at a certain time. The captain and the spy, who had already discovered so much, were to seek out the house and arrange some plan for attacking it.

This they did without delay, but when the captain and the spy came to the street in which Ali Baba lived, they could not tell which was the right house, since they found a number of doors marked with chalk in the same way. The spy was full of dismay when he saw what a trick had been played upon him, and, fearing the captain's anger, he declared that he had marked only one of the doors, and had quite expected to know the house again by means of that mark. But the captain only led the way to the great square where the other robbers were already waiting; and telling them that their plan had completely failed, he said they must return to the forest, for they could do nothing more that day.

When the robbers were once more safe in their cave, they killed the spy who had failed in his work; and then, as their danger was as great as ever, another of the troop offered to seek out their enemy's house, although the captain promised that he also should die if he failed as the other had done. This second offer was gladly accepted and the new spy set out.

He went straight to Baba Mustapha's stall, and, by giving him plenty of gold, persuaded the old cobbler to be blindfolded once more, and to lead the way to Ali Baba's house. When they arrived there the robber took a piece of red chalk he had brought with him, and marked the door in an out-of-the-way place, feeling sure he would thus know it again; and then he let the cobbler go back to his stall, and returned to the forest cave.

When the second spy declared that he could certainly point out the house where their enemy lived, the robbers were pleased, and decided to enter the town again in the same manner as before. But when the captain and the spy came into the street they were once more disappointed, for Morgiana's keen eyes had noticed the red chalk mark on her master's door, and by carefully marking the neighbouring doors in exactly the same way and place with red chalk also, she had again spoilt the robber's plan.

The captain and his men returned to the forest in an awful rage, and when they got to their cave they quickly killed the second spy for having failed in his task.

Now, the robber captain, not wishing to lose any more of

his fine troop in this way, said that he himself would go alone into the town and see if he could succeed better; so he disguised himself and set off.

As the other spies had done, he went to the old cobbler, Baba Mustapha, who, for the sake of more gold, was willing to be blindfolded once again and to lead the robber to Ali Baba's house. When he got there the captain did not mark the door at all, but looked well at the house, noting exactly at what part of the street it lay, and walking past it many times, so that he knew he could not fail to find it when next he came.

Then he went back to the cave and told his men that he had thought of a fine plan for doing away with their enemy, and he bade them go in small parties into the villages round about, and buy nineteen mules and thirty-eight very large leather jars, one of which was to be full of oil, and the rest to be empty.

In a few days the mules and jars were all bought, and then the captain set to work to carry out the plan he had thought of. He put a robber into each of the empty leather jars, rubbing the outsides with oil, and covering over the tops, but leaving a little opening for air to get in, and then he loaded each mule with two of the jars, one on either side, taking care to carry the jar of real oil with him as well, in case anyone might wish to look at his goods.

When all was ready, he dressed himself up as a merchant and set out with his loaded mules, arriving in the town just as it was growing dusk. He led them on purpose through the street where his enemy lived, and when he came up to the right house he was pleased to find Ali Baba himself sitting outside the door, enjoying the cool evening air.

He at once left his mules and went to speak to Ali Baba, saying that he was a merchant and had brought oil from a great distance to sell in the market next day, but that it was now so late he did not care to go farther into the town; and he asked Ali Baba if he might pass the night with him.

Ali Baba did not recognize the disguised robber-captain,

but thinking that the stranger before him was a respectable oil merchant, he said he was welcome to spend the night with him; and he at once sent a slave to lead the mules into the yard at the back of the house, and to unload them there, whilst he himself went to Morgiana to bid her get ready a good supper for his guest. At first the sham merchant did not wish to enter Ali Baba's house, thinking he might carry out his plan better if he passed the night in the yard; but Ali Baba would not hear of this, and so he was obliged to do as his host wished.

A fine supper was quickly served, and whilst his guest feasted, Ali Baba talked pleasantly to him; but at last he went away to say something to Morgiana, and at the same time the robber captain stepped into the yard to look at his mules, so he said, but really to speak to his men. He warned them that when they heard him throw some stones into the yard from his chamber window at a certain time during the night, they were to cut open with their knives the leather bags in which they were hidden, to step out, and wait until he joined them. When he had whispered these directions into each jar, he returned to the house, and Morgiana took him to the room where he was to sleep. This room, as it happened, overlooked the yard.

Now, Ali Baba had told Morgiana that as he intended to go to the baths very early next morning, she was to put out his bathing garments ready for him, and to make him some nice broth to take when he returned. Before going to rest, the careful slave did what her master bade her. She put out the bathing garments, and began to make the broth; but while she was doing this the lamp went out, and since there was no more oil in the house she did not know how she would finish her work.

The man-slave, Abdalla, seeing what a fix she was in, told her to go into the yard and take a little oil from one of the great jars the merchant had brought. So Morgiana, thinking this to be good advice, took her oil-pot and went out into the yard. But great was her surprise on reaching the first jar to hear a voice from within say these words in a very soft tone: "Is it time?"

Now, most maidens would have screamed and made a great fuss on finding a man in a jar which was supposed to be full of oil. But Morgiana was wise and not easily frightened, and, understanding at once that she had surprised some secret that meant danger to her master's household, she kept quiet and answered in an equally low tone: "Not yet, but presently!" She then went to each of the jars in turn, and whispered the same answer, until she came to the last, which she found to be full of oil.

Having discovered that a band of robbers were in the yard, only waiting for word from their leader, the supposed merchant, to do some dreadful deed, Morgiana felt that her beloved master and his household were in great danger, and that it rested with her alone to save them, since everyone else was in bed. She, therefore, made up her mind to lose no time, and thought out a clever plan.

Very quickly she made up a big fire in the kitchen, and taking her largest kettle, she filled it with oil from the jar outside, and put it on to boil. As soon as it was ready, she took the kettle into the yard, and quickly poured just enough of the boiling oil into each of the jars to kill the man inside. She did this so suddenly and so quietly that the robbers had not time to call out before they were smothered, and so no noise was made. After preparing her master's broth, Morgiana put out the lights, and waited to see what would happen next.

In a short time she saw the pretended merchant, whom she now knew to be the captain of the thieves, come to his chamber window, and throw some pebbles on to the jars in the yard. He did this several times. Finding that his men did not stir, he grew alarmed, and crept softly down into the yard to see what was the matter. He looked into each of the jars, and saw that all his men were dead. He smelt the boiling oil that had been poured over them, and knew that his fine plan for destroying and robbing Ali Baba and his household had been found out and spoilt. Full of rage, he made his way into the garden, and escaped over the walls.

When Morgiana saw that the robber captain was now safely out of the way, she herself went to rest, without saying a word to anyone of what had happened.

Next morning, when Ali Baba returned from the baths, he was surprised to find the jars of oil still in the yard, for he had expected that the merchant would have gone at daybreak, so as to be early at the market. So he asked Morgiana what this meant.

Morgiana took her master into the yard, and showing him the dead men in the jars, told him the whole story of the wicked plot she had discovered and spoilt. She also told him for the first time about the chalk marks she had seen before on the door, and which she now knew to be connected with this plot of the forest robbers.

When Ali Baba heard this strange story, he was full of surprise. He felt so grateful to Morgiana, who by her cleverness and bravery had saved his life and the lives of all his household, that he decided that, as a reward for what she had done, she should be a slave no longer. He then called Abdalla, and the two of them set to work to bury the dead robbers secretly in the garden, that no one might know of the strange thing that had happened. By selling the mules at different times, and living in a quiet manner, he prevented people from talking about him, and from guessing how he became rich in so short a time.

In the meantime, the robber captain went back to his cave, angry because his plan had failed, and full of grief at the loss of his companions. He wondered how he would ever manage to get such a fine troop of men together again; but before seeking out a new band to guard his treasures, he made up his mind to try once more to destroy Ali Baba, who he felt would be a danger to him as long as he lived, since he knew the secret of the cave.

So, next day, he disguised himself again, and carrying a number of rich silks and stuffs with him, he went into the town; and taking a lodging and warehouse, he began business as a cloth merchant, under the false name of Cogia Houssain. The warehouse he had taken was next door to that in which Ali Baba's son did business, and he had chosen it for this very reason; for he hoped to become friendly with the young man, and to use him in carrying out his evil plan.

By behaving well and being pleasant, the supposed merchant, Cogia Houssain, soon became very friendly with all the people round about, and especially with Ali Baba's son, whom he treated most kindly, often inviting him to dine at his house, and loading him with favours; so much so, indeed, that the young man was eager to make some return to his new friend. He spoke to his father about this, saying he would like to invite Cogia Houssain to dine with him, but that his own house was not large or fine enough to entertain such a guest in the way he wished. Then Ali Baba said that he himself would be glad to receive his son's friend, and advised him to walk out with Cogia Houssain some time, and call in on their way back, as this would look more friendly than sending him a formal invitation.

On the following day, the young man asked Cogia Houssain to walk out with him; and when they came to Ali Baba's house, he asked the merchant to enter, saying his father was most eager to know him. The robber, though he meant to enter this house and kill his enemy some time or other, had not yet made his plans, and so did not wish to accept the invitation; but Ali Baba's son would not hear of him going away, and, taking him by the hand, insisted on bringing him into his father's house.

Ali Baba received his son's friend with great favour, and said that he must remain to supper; but the false merchant asked to be excused, saying he had a good reason for not staying to supper. When he was asked to state his reason, he said that he could not eat any food with salt in it; but Ali Baba said that this did not matter, for he would give orders that no salt should be put into the food that would be served for supper.

Now, it is a custom in the East, where the scene of this

story is laid, for one who has eaten of another's salt to be obliged to be friendly to that person, and to do well by him; and so the robber captain thought that if he ate salt in Ali Baba's house, he could not then kill him, since he would feel obliged to treat him well. But, of course, Ali Baba did not know the real reason why his guest did not wish to eat salt just then, and thought it was only because it did not agree with him. So, without thinking any more about the matter, he went and told Morgiana to be sure not to put any salt in the supper she was getting ready, for his guest did not like it. Morgiana, however, was not so easily satisfied, and as she was laying the dishes on the supper-table, she took a good look at the strange guest who would not eat salt in her master's house. Although Cogia Houssain was so well disguised, she knew him at once to be the robber captain, whose plan she had caused to fail before; and seeing also that he had a dagger hidden inside his garments, she guessed that he meant to kill Ali Baba, and quickly thought of a way to prevent him a second time from doing this wicked deed.

When she had put all things on the table ready for supper, she left the three men to their feast; and without telling her master what she had discovered, she at once set off to carry out the plan she had made.

Morgiana was right in thinking that the robber captain meant to kill her master; for, since chance had brought him into Ali Baba's house sooner than he had expected, he made up his mind to destroy his enemy now that he was brought face to face with him. He was just thinking, when supper was over, how he would be able to do this without any danger to himself, when Morgiana with some musicians entered the room again.

Morgiana had dressed herself very prettily as a dancer, and round her waist she wore a silver girdle, into which she had thrust a scimitar; and she had brought the musicians with her that she might dance before her master's guest.

As soon as Ali Baba saw Morgiana, he was pleased, and

called upon her to amuse them with her dancing; but the robber captain was not so pleased, for he saw that he would now have to wait a longer time before he could carry out his evil plan.

However, he pretended to be pleased, and so the dance began, the musicians playing a lively tune.

Now, Morgiana was a very good dancer, and had often won great praise from her master's guests by her graceful movements; but never had she danced so well as she did on this night. Her last dance was best of all; for, drawing a scimitar from her girdle, she held it high over her head, and went through many wild and strange movements; but just as Ali Baba was admiring her skill more than he had ever done before, he saw her, to his horror, plunge the scimitar into the heart of Cogia Houssain, who fell over dead!

Very much shocked, Ali Baba demanded why she had thus killed the guest beneath his roof; and then Morgiana explained how she had discovered that Cogia Houssain was really the robber captain, and pointed out the dagger which he had hidden beneath his garment.

When Ali Baba heard this, and saw for himself that it was indeed the robber captain who had been his guest, and that Morgiana had again saved his life, he felt more grateful than ever to her. He promised not only that she should be a free maiden, but also that she should be married to his son, and so become a great lady.

Ali Baba's son was only too willing to make Morgiana his bride, for, besides being beautiful, he knew her to be brave, good, and clever; so, a few days later, they were married, and a grand feast was held in their honour.

For long Ali Baba forbore from going again to the robbers' cave. But at the year's end when he found no further attempt was made on his life, he had the curiosity to make another journey there. When he found that nobody had been there since the false Cogia Houssain he did not doubt that he was the only person in the world to know the secret cave.

Thereafter Ali Baba had the secret of the treasure cave all

to himself and his family; and since the secret was most carefully kept, he lived a rich man for the rest of his life. As for his son and the beautiful Morgiana, they grew to love each other so well that it would not have been possible to find a happier pair in all the world.

The Merchant and the Genie

A rich merchant was once obliged to take a long journey across a lonely desert; and feeling very hot and tired one day, he stopped to rest for a short time beneath some shady trees, where a fountain of clear water played.

Having tied his horse to a tree, he sat down on the grass, and took some biscuits and dates out of a bag he had with him; and as he ate the dates he carelessly threw the stones about with a good deal of force.

When he had finished his meal, he prepared to go on his journey once more; but just as he was about to set off, a monstrous genie suddenly appeared, and, brandishing a great scimitar in his hand, said in a dreadful voice:

"Rise up, that I may slay you!"

"But what have I done?" cried the terrified merchant

"You have killed my son!" shrieked the angry genie. "He was flying, invisible, past this fountain just now, and was slain by the date stones you flung aside so wildly!"

Full of dismay, the frightened merchant begged for mercy; and when the genie still refused to allow him to live, he added: "Grant me at least another year of life, that I may bid farewell to my family and settle my affairs; and I promise you I will return to this same spot at the end of that time, when you may do with me what you will!"

After much persuasion the genie agreed to this. "But," he added sternly, "do not hope to escape me; for, should you fail to return at the exact time appointed, I shall soon seek you out!"

The genie then vanished, and the merchant, mounting his horse in haste went on with his journey. When he arrived home, his wife and children were shocked to find him so dull and sad, and when he had told them of the promise he had given to the genie, they were full of grief.

The merchant, however, knew there was no way of escape for him; so he set to work to settle all his affairs. When at last the year came to an end, he bade a sorrowful farewell to his wife and children; and then he mounted his horse and set off on his sad journey.

When he arrived at the fountain in the desert, an old man leading a hind came by, and asked him why he chose to rest in that lonely place. The merchant told him of his meeting with the genie, and of the promise he had been compelled to give; and whilst they were talking, another old man came towards them, followed by two black dogs. The old man with the hind told him of the merchant's sad state; and soon afterwards a third old man came by, to whom they told the same story.

Whilst the three old men were vainly trying to cheer the merchant with their talk, the terrible genie suddenly appeared in a thick cloud of vapour, with a drawn scimitar in his hand. He at once seized the trembling merchant by the arm, and said in a voice of thunder: "Get up, that I may kill you as you have killed my son!"

On hearing these dreadful words, the old man with the hind threw himself at the genie's feet, and said:

"Powerful Genie, stay your hand, I pray. Let me tell you the strange story of my life and of this hind; and if you think it wonderful, I hope you will pardon this unhappy merchant at least a third of his crime on that account."

The genie, who loved to listen to a good story, agreed to this, and the old man began at once.

"Sir," he said to the genie, "this hind you see is really my wife. She was a very beautiful lady when I married her, and for many years we lived happily together. Then, as we had no children, I took another wife, by whom I had a son; and from this time my first wife seemed to change. Although I did not love her any less than before, she grew jealous of the natural affection I had for my young son; and, as the years went on, she grew to hate him, and also his mother, so intensely that at length she resolved to kill them both, taking care, however, to lay her plans so cleverly that she should not be found out.

"When my son had grown to be a very promising youth, it happened that I had to undertake a very long journey, which kept me from home for a year; and as soon as I had set off on my travels, my wife began to carry out her wicked plans. She first of all set herself to study magic; and then, having learnt sufficient of the black art for her purpose, she changed my son into a calf, and his mother into a cow, handing them both over to my head farmer to fatten for sacrifice. When I returned home, she told me that my second wife had died during my absence, and that my son had been lost for many months. I was much grieved at this sad news, but I still hoped that my son would return.

"A few weeks later a grand sacred festival was being held, and in honour of the event I gave orders to my farmer to bring me a fine fat cow to sacrifice. The cow he brought me happened to be my transformed wife; and as I bound her, ready for sacrifice, she bellowed loudly, and, to my surprise, I saw tears streaming from her eyes. I felt strangely full of pity for the poor creature, and declared I could not sacrifice her; but my first wife, seeing her wicked plans about to fall to the ground, urged me to continue my work, and not withhold such a worthy offering from the festival.

"So I took up the knife once more; but again the cow's tears streamed down so piteously that I could not proceed, and so bade my farmer to sacrifice her, which he did without further delay. I then ordered him to bring me the fattest calf he had, which happened to be my poor son. To my utter astonishment, directly the calf saw me, it broke from its cord and bounded to my side, rubbing its head lovingly against me, and looking up into my face with appealing eyes streaming with tears.

"Feeling greatly moved, and quite unable to sacrifice the gentle creature, I was about to return it to the farmer, when my wife, full of rage, scornfully upbraided me for being so childish; and, to please her, I again took up the knife. But the poor calf's tears were more than I could bear, and, in spite of my wife's scolding, I decided to have another creature to sacrifice, and so gave the calf back into the hands of the farmer, bidding him take great care of it, since its strange conduct interested me.

"Next day the farmer came to me in haste, saying that his young daughter, who had studied magic for the purpose of doing good, had discovered by her arts that the calf I had spared was none other than my son, who had been changed into that form by the evil spells of my jealous wife, who had also changed his mother into the cow which had unfortunately been sacrificed on the day before.

"Full of amazement at this story I at once visited the farmer's daughter, and asked if she knew sufficient magic to bring my son back into his natural form. She replied that her knowledge of the art was quite sufficient for this purpose; but she declared that she would only work the charm on condition that I allowed her to marry my son when she had restored him, and also to punish my wife for her wickedness by treating her in the same way as she had treated her two victims. As the young girl was fair and charming, I agreed to her terms; and then, by means of a magic spell, she restored my son to his proper form. When I had gladly embraced my dear son, I presented him to his benefactress, saying that I desired him to marry her, since he owed so much to her; and the youth, having instantly fallen in love with the beautiful maiden, very joyfully consented. They were married very shortly afterwards, and then, by exerting her magic still further, the young bride changed my wife into this hind, which you see before you. Wherever I go on my travels this hind goes with me; and that is how she comes to be in this wild place.

"This is my story, O Genie; and if it has pleased you, I beg that you will give me the reward I asked."

The genie declared that the story had been an excellent one; and he said that, as he had promised, he would forgive the merchant a third part of his crime.

On hearing this, the second old man, with the two black dogs, came forward, and said that if the genie would forgive the merchant another third of his misdeed, he would tell him a more wonderful story still; and when the genie had also agreed to this, he began at once.

"Great Genie, these two black dogs are my brothers! When my father died, he left us each a thousand sequins; and with this money we all set up in business. Some time afterwards my eldest brother sold his share in the business, and with the money thus raised bought goods, and set off to seek his fortunes by travel. He remained away for a whole year, and at the end of that time he returned as a beggar, and implored my help, since he had lost all his money by bad trading, and had now nothing to live upon. I at once took him into my house, and gave him of the best food and clothing I had; and then, finding that I was by this time worth two thousand sequins, I gave him one thousand with which to make a fresh start. With this he retrieved his fortunes, and we all lived together as before.

"A short time afterwards my second brother sold his share in the business, and went to travel for a year; but at the end of that time he also returned as a beggar, having lost all his fortune likewise. I received him kindly, and, having again been successful in my own business, I gave him another thousand sequins, with which he was able to begin afresh as a merchant.

"For a little time we all lived comfortably together; and then my two brothers suggested that we should undertake a voyage, and go trading to other countries. For a long while I refused to join in their enterprise; but at length they overcame my objections, and I agreed to go with them. When the time came to stock our ship, I found to my surprise that my brothers had again lost the money I had given them, and had nothing to pay towards the expenses of our voyage; but I once more bore patiently with their carelessness, and having by this time increased my own fortune to six thousand sequins, I divided the half equally amongst us, and buried the remaining three thousand in a corner of my house.

"Having fully stocked our ship, we set sail; and having journeyed to many distant ports, we did excellent business. I, myself, was even more successful than my brothers, gaining ten times what I had ventured. Having completed our business, we prepared to return home; but, before embarking, I met with an adventure. As I was walking along the seashore a strange lady of great beauty, but clad in poor, ragged garments, came up to me and implored me to marry her. For some time I firmly refused; but at last her entreaties prevailed, for she was fair to look upon, and she persisted that it was my duty to marry her, because she was so poor and friendless, declaring that if I would agree to marry her, I should never regret it, since she would certainly prove of great service to me. So I granted her request; and having married her at once, and provided her with handsome clothing, we embarked with my brothers without further delay. On the voyage I found that my wife was as good as she was beautiful, and I grew to love her more dearly every day; and very soon I had cause to be grateful to her. My two brothers, always envious of my good fortune, now allowed their unjust jealousy to get the better of them; and so, being eager to have all my wealth for themselves, they seized my wife and myself as we lay sleeping one night, and threw us both into the sea.

"Fortunately for me, my wife proved to be a fairy; and so, by her magic, she was able to save us both and bring us to land. She then told me that, having seen me on the seashore, she had fallen in love with me at once; but, in order to prove my goodness of heart, she had disguised herself as a poor woman, to see if I would show pity upon one who appeared to be so unfortunate. Having thus won my love, and proved to her own satisfaction that I was of a kindly nature, she had gladly used her magic in my behalf; but she now declared her anger was so great against my two false brothers that she was determined to kill them. After a great deal of persuasion on my part, however, she finally agreed to spare their lives, and to punish them in some other way; and then, having by means of her magic transported me to my own house once more, she suddenly disappeared. I entered the house, and having dug up the three thousand sequins I had buried, I opened my shop again and soon began to do a brisk business.

"On returning to the house I was met by these two black dogs, who came and licked my hands; and presently my fairy-wife appeared also, saying that the dogs were my two brothers, whom she had thus transformed because of their evil conduct to me, and whom she had condemned to remain in this shape for ten years, at the end of which time she would restore them if I sought her out. Having told me where to seek her, and bidding me an affectionate farewell (for, being a fairy, she could not remain with me always), she suddenly vanished; and as the ten years are now nearly at an end, I am travelling in search of her, that my repentant brothers may regain their proper forms.

"This is my story, O Genie; and if you think it wonderful, I pray that you will pardon this poor merchant another third of his crime."

The genie declared that the story had been very entertaining, and that he would certainly grant the teller's request; and, upon hearing this, the third old man came forward and said that if the great one would pardon the remaining third of the merchant's misdeed he would tell him of adventures even stranger than any that had yet been told. His request having also been granted he began at once; and the story he told was so truly amazing that when it came to an end the genie gladly agreed to forgive the merchant the last third of his crime, declaring that he had never been so well entertained before.

Having spoken thus, the genie instantly vanished in a cloud of vapour; and, full of joy, the merchant embraced the three old men, and gratefully thanked them for having so cleverly saved his life. His new friends declared they were only too glad to have been of use to one so full of woe, and bidding him farewell they went on their way.

Then the merchant returned to his home, where he was received with the greatest joy; and he spent the rest of his life with his wife and children in peace and happiness.

The Enchanted Horse

In the country of Persia New Year's Day, which occurs at the beginning of Spring, is kept as a very great festival, when all kinds of rejoicings and gay doings take place, not only in the large cities, but also in the small towns and even in villages. But it is at the king's court that the most splendid entertainments are held; and strangers and visitors from all parts are invited to the capital to see and admire the wonderful objects of art and the strange inventions brought before the king and his court at such times.

It was on one of these great festival days that a very strange thing happened.

The Royal Court was at that time held in the city of Schiraz, and the king and his lords were assembled in one of the large squares, admiring the many beautiful and wonderful things brought for them to see. After having bestowed great praise and rewards upon the artists and the inventors, they were just about to return to the palace, when a Hindu suddenly appeared with an artificial horse, very richly arrayed, and so wonderfully well imitated that at first sight the people thought it to be a live animal.

The Hindu bowed low before the king, and then said:

"Though I come last before your majesty, I am sure that nothing you have yet seen is more wonderful than this horse of mine, at which I now beg of you to look!"

The king replied that he saw nothing wonderful about the horse, except that it was very well imitated, and that his own workmen could do the same The Hindu then said:

"Your majesty, it is not for his outward form that my horse is so wonderful, but for the secret power within him. Whenever I mount him, he will instantly carry me through the air to any part of the world where I may wish to find myself. I shall be pleased to show you this wonder, if your majesty will but command me to do so."

Now, the King of Persia was very fond of anything strange or curious, and though he could scarcely believe that the Hindu's imitation horse could really have such marvellous powers, he was very eager to prove whether he spoke the truth or not; and so, at his request, the Hindu mounted his strange steed with ease, and, when seated, asked the king where he wished to send him.

The king pointed towards a certain high mountain in the distance, which could just be seen from the square, and said: "Do you see that mountain? It is not a great way off, but quite far enough for me to judge of the speed you can make in going and in coming. Go to it, and bring me back a branch of the palm-tree growing at the foot of it!"

No sooner had the king spoken than the Hindu turned a peg in the neck of his steed, and instantly the horse rose into the air and carried him out of sight with the quickness of lightning, to the great amazement of the king and the people gathered in the square.

In a few minutes, as they still gazed in wonder, they saw him returning with the palm branch in his hand. The horse gave a few turns in the air, and then alighted on the ground, in the same place from which he had started; and the Hindu, jumping off and bowing before the king, laid the palm branch at his feet.

The King of Persia was now so delighted with the wonderful horse that he longed to have it for his own, to place amongst his other curious treasures; and he eagerly asked the Hindu what price he would take for it.

The Hindu said that though he knew the horse would bring him great fame in the world, nevertheless he was willing to part with it if the king was ready to pay him the price he wanted for his treasure.

The king said he was willing to pay any reasonable price which he might ask, and even offered to give him one of his richest cities to reign over as king; but the Hindu said he did not care about such an offer, and that he would part with his precious horse only on condition that the King of Persia gave him his daughter's hand in marriage.

The lords and the people standing around began to laugh at the idea of such a person being married to their royal princess; but the king himself, longing more than ever to possess the magic horse, was quiet, thinking whether he might not pay even such an unheard-of price as this, in order to obtain his wish.

However, his eldest son, Prince Firouz Schah, a handsome, noble-hearted young man, was very indignant with the Hindu for daring to ask such a thing. He begged of his royal father not to think for a moment of giving the princess, his sister, in marriage to a mere low-born Hindu juggler, who was certainly not fit to enter their noble family.

But the king said he would not like the Hindu to sell his horse to another king, who might then boast of owning a greater treasure than he himself could show, and that he hoped yet to satisfy the Hindu with something other than his royal daughter's hand in marriage. In the meantime he asked the prince to try the horse himself, and to give him his opinion of its strange powers.

The young prince saw no harm in doing this; so he quickly mounted the horse, and, without waiting for the Hindu to tell him how to work it, he turned the peg in its neck, and it instantly rose off the ground and carried him out of sight in a few moments, to the alarm of the king, who had not expected his son to act so hastily.

The Hindu, afraid of the king's anger, at once fell on his

knees before him, saying he was not to blame if any accident happened, since the young prince had not waited for his advice and directions about the horse, and would not therefore know how to make it return to earth.

On hearing in what danger his son was from not knowing how to guide the horse, the king was in great grief, and he angrily ordered his soldiers to keep the Hindu in prison, saying that if the prince did not return safe and sound his head would be cut off. Then he returned to the palace, and the great feast-day ended in sorrow and dismay.

Meanwhile Prince Firouz Schah, on the back of the Enchanted Horse, was being carried forward through the air at a dreadful rate, mounting higher and higher until he could see nothing down below; and though he had been eager enough to begin such a wonderful ride, he soon wished to return. He now found how foolish he had been not to wait for the Hindu's directions before starting off; for though he turned the peg backwards and forwards many times, the horse still went forward, mounting higher and higher, and he knew there must be some secret spring he did not know of, to make it return to earth.

Much alarmed at the danger he was in, he quickly took a careful look all over the horse's head and neck; and presently noticing another peg behind the right ear, he turned it, and to his joy found that this caused the horse to return towards the earth, rather more slowly than it had arisen.

The horse had now travelled a great distance, and it was night-time in that part of the world over which it bore the prince, who was in some fear lest he should be dropped into a desert or into the middle of the ocean; but at last, to his great relief, he felt the Enchanted Horse stop, just about midnight, and rest upon something solid and firm.

Prince Firouz Schah at once stepped on to the ground, feeling very tired, dizzy, and hungry. To his surprise he found himself on the terrace of a splendid palace, with a balustrade of beautiful shining white marble all around it. After groping about in the dark for a time, he came to a staircase which led down into a room, through the open door of which there came a glimmer of light; and, without stopping to think of possible dangers, he crept softly down the steps, and found himself in a great hall, where a number of black slaves lay sleeping with drawn sabres in their hands, before the open doorway of another room from which a light streamed forth.

The sight of these great black slaves was enough to let Prince Firouz Schah know that he was near the sleeping-chamber of some royal princess, over whom they were keeping guard; and stepping very lightly up to the chamber beyond, he drew aside the silken curtain, and stepped inside without awakening the blacks.

He saw that it was indeed the sleeping-room of some princess, for a number of ladies-in-waiting were lying asleep on couches a little apart from their royal mistress, who also lay sleeping on a richly-draped sofa.

The prince, without casting a glance at the other ladies, went straight up to the couch of the princess, and there he beheld a maiden so wonderfully beautiful that he fell in love with her at first sight. He quickly stooped over the couch, and, touching the sleeve of the princess's robe, he very gently awakened her.

When the princess opened her eyes she was astonished to see a handsome stranger gazing down upon her, and the prince, without giving her time to speak or to call out in alarm, bowed low, and at once began to tell her how he came to be there at such a time.

He explained that he was the son of the King of Persia, and that it was owing to a most strange event that happened at a festival held yesterday that he now found himself in a country the name of which he knew not. He was afraid that he might not be well received by the people, and he begged the princess to help him, since she was surely much too beautiful to be unkind.

The princess, who was really the daughter of the King of Bengal, a country of India, was quite charmed with the handsome young prince before her, and promised at once to protect and help him; and, though she was most eager to hear the story of his strange adventure, she saw from his tired looks that he must first of all rest and refresh himself, so she gave orders to her ladies, who were now awake and were gazing in amazement at the stranger, to take the prince at once to another room, where, after having some food, he could rest until morning.

The attendants quickly arose, and taking lighted candles in their hands they led the prince to a splendid sleeping-chamber, where, after bringing him a hasty meal, they left him to rest. On their return to the princess they told her, in answer to her eager questions, that they thought the stranger quite the most delightful young prince in the world, and they hoped she might be allowed to marry him.

Next morning the Princess of Bengal took a longer time to dress than she had ever done before, and was most particular to be arrayed in her richest robes and most dazzling jewels; and when she was at last ready she went to visit her guest of the night before.

Prince Firouz Schah, greatly refreshed after his sleep, was quite ready to receive the princess; and finding that she was most eager to hear of his adventures, he told her the whole story of the New Year Festival and of the Enchanted Horse that had brought him so unexpectedly to her palace. He said how surprised he had been to find himself set down outside a palace (which he had since learned was in India), and how he had made his way to her room; and he ended his story by declaring that her wonderful beauty and kindness had already filled his heart with such a great love that he was ready to serve her as a slave.

The Princess of Bengal trembled with alarm on hearing of the dangers her royal guest had just gone through, but she was greatly pleased with his last words (for she had never met with a more delightful young prince), though she said she had no idea of making a slave of him, since she wished him to feel quite free and happy whilst he remained in her palace.

She then led the prince to a splendid hall, where a rich meal was set out, and whilst they ate and talked a delightful concert of the sweetest music was gone through by a number of beautiful and richly-dressed slaves. After this the princess showed her guest the chief sights of the handsome summer-palace she was now staying in, which was in the country, away from the capital; and although the prince admired the buildings and the gardens very greatly she told him that the royal palace of her father, the King of Bengal, was much more rich and splendid, and she hoped he would visit it presently, since she felt sure her father would receive him with great honour and kindness.

But Prince Firouz Schah said that much as he would like to remain and visit the King of Bengal, he felt he must not do so, since his own father, the King of Persia, would be longing for his return, not knowing whether he were alive or dead.

On hearing this the princess said she did not wish to keep her guest from doing what he felt to be his duty, and saw she must not expect him to visit the royal palace of Bengal at present; but being alarmed at the thought that he meant to leave her so soon, and fearing lest he might forget her when once more safely home, she begged of him to make at least a little longer stay with herself, that they might learn to know each other better.

After the great kindness to him the young prince felt that he could not refuse her request, besides which he really longed to remain, as his love for her grew deeper as each moment went by; so he gladly accepted her invitation, and the princess at once began to make all kinds of pleasant plans for his amusement.

Every day there were delightful concerts and splendid feasts in the palace gardens, or gay hunting-parties; and when tired after these pleasures, the Prince of Persia and Princess of Bengal would meet in a certain beautiful spot in the gardens, where they could rest as they talked of all kinds of pleasant things. The prince would talk of the richness and splendours of his own country of Persia, and the princess would talk of the beauties of Bengal; and at the end of two months, which flew away all too quickly in this delightful manner, they had grown to know and love one another very well.

But now Prince Firouz Schah declared that he really must not stay any longer, and begged the princess to allow him to go back to his father, promising that he would quickly return in truly princely style to ask for her hand in marriage from the King of Bengal; and then, seeing that she seemed very sad at the idea of his leaving her, and might be even doubting whether he would really return, he begged of her to go with him to Persia on the Enchanted Horse, and be presented to his father.

The Princess of Bengal, being indeed downcast at the thought of parting from her handsome young prince, was full of joy at his last request; and when he declared that he now understood how to manage the wonderful horse, she was quite willing to go with him.

So, early the next morning, whilst all in the palace were still asleep, the prince and princess met on the marble terrace, and mounted the Enchanted Horse, without anyone seeing what they were about; and then the prince, after seeing that the princess was safely seated with her arms round his waist, turned the peg, and the horse at once rose up into the air, and flew at a great rate towards Persia.

On nearing Schiraz the prince guided the horse to a pleasure-palace just outside the city, and when they had alighted, he left the princess there in charge of the attendants, saying he would return for her when he had told the king of her arrival; and then, having put the Enchanted Horse in a place of safety, he mounted one of his own royal steeds, and rode off into the city towards his father's palace.

The people in the streets, on seeing their beloved young prince, whom they had believed to be dead, riding past alive and well, set up great cheers of delight; and when he reached the palace he was received by his father with every mark of love and gladness.

After rejoicing over his dear son's return for some time, the King of Persia presently asked him what had become of the Hindu's wonderful horse; and then Prince Firouz Schah told the whole story of his adventures, ending up by asking his father's consent to his marriage with the beautiful Princess of Bengal, whom he had brought back with him on the Enchanted Horse.

The King of Persia was only too willing for his son to marry a princess of so rich and powerful a country as Bengal then was, and he at once gave orders that a grand procession, which he and the prince would themselves head, should be got ready to go and bring her into the city.

He also caused the Hindu, who had been kept in prison all this time, to be now set free; and on his being first of all brought into his presence, he told him to leave the country at once, and take his magic horse with him, since it had already done enough mischief.

Now, the Hindu was really wicked and cruel; and being very angry at having been kept in prison and refused what he had desired, he quickly thought of an evil plan, by means of which he could revenge himself upon the King and the Prince of Persia.

On leaving the king's palace, where all were busy making ready to go and fetch the Princess of Bengal, he hurried secretly to the pleasure-palace outside the city, and demanded to see the chief attendants at once. When they appeared, he said he had been sent by the King and Prince of Persia to bring the Princess of Bengal into the city on the Enchanted Horse, and set her down in the great square, where the royal court waited to receive her, that all the people might behold the wonderful sight.

The palace-keeper, seeing that the Hindu was free and evidently in favour once again, believed that he spoke the truth; and when the princess heard that he had been sent by the Prince of Persia to fetch her, she was quite ready to go with him.

So the Enchanted Horse was brought out, and the princess placed on it. Then the Hindu, well pleased at the success of his wicked plan, sprang up beside her, and turned the peg, and the horse began to mount into the air.

It was just at this moment that the splendid royal procession, with the King and Prince of Persia at its head, arrived in the great square of the city, on their way to fetch the Princess of Bengal; and, to make his revenge more complete, the Hindu guided the Enchanted Horse over their heads, that all might see the prize which he was taking away with him.

The King of Persia, on seeing what a wicked trick had been played upon them all, shouted to the Hindu to stop at once, and called him every bad name he could think of; but the Hindu only laughed with scorn, and, clutching his prize more tightly, made the Enchanted Horse rise at a terrific rate, so that in a few moments it vanished out of sight.

Poor Prince Firouz Schah was full of grief at seeing his beautiful princess, whom he so dearly loved, so suddenly snatched away from him by the wicked Hindu juggler; but he would not quite give himself up to despair, so instead of joining the now mournful procession back to the king's palace, he set off quickly towards the pleasure-palace outside the city, from which his dear princess had just been stolen.

The palace-keeper, on seeing the prince, fell on his knees, declaring he was not to blame for the dreadful thing that had happened; but the prince, instead of being angry, only desired that he would fetch him the clothes of a dervish, or Mohammedan monk. In a short time the keeper returned with the robe of a dervish; and when he had put this on, the prince, taking with him a box of rich jewels he had meant to present to his bride, left the palace, and began a long, weary journey in search of his lost princess, making up his mind not to return home until he had found her.

In the meantime the clever Hindu quickly bore his prize to a great distance; and when evening fell, he guided the Enchanted Horse to a wood near the chief city of Kashmir in India, where he alighted and went in search of some food.

The poor Princess of Bengal, who had soon found out what a wicked creature held her in his power, was quite overcome with grief, fearing that she would never see her dear prince again; but she quickly made up her mind to try and escape from the cruel Hindu as soon as ever she could.

She would have crept away at once whilst she was alone in the woods, but found herself too faint and weary to do so; but when the Hindu presently returned with food, she ate some of it, hoping to get back strength enough to carry out a plan of escape.

However, she soon found that he did not mean to give her any chance of getting away, but intended to keep her as a slave for himself. After many threats, she saw that he was about to ill-treat her, and he began to beat her so badly that she cried out for help.

Fortunately her cries were heard by a party of horsemen, who quickly rode up to see what was the matter. This party turned out to be the Sultan of Kashmir and his lords, who were just returning from a hunt; and, seeing that a quarrel was taking place, the sultan demanded to know what it was all about.

The Hindu, on being asked why he ill-treated the lady with him, replied that she was his wife and slave; but the Princess of Bengal, full of indignation, said this was not true, since she was a princess, who would scorn to be married to such a base creature, and that the Hindu was a wicked magician who had stolen her away from the Prince of Persia, and brought her to this wood on an Enchanted Horse, which stood near by.

The Sultan of Kashmir was so moved by the tears and the cries of the poor princess, and was so pleased with her wonderful beauty, that he was quite ready to help and protect her; and he quickly ordered his guards to seize the Hindu and cut off his head that instant.

When this was done he brought the princess to his palace, where she was put into a splendid room, with a great number of slaves to wait upon her. The poor princess was glad to rest once more and be treated so kindly; but next day her troubles began again, and she found that she was not much better off than before.

The sultan was so delighted with her beauty and charming manners that, instead of returning her to the Prince of Persia, as she so much desired, he made up his mind to keep her in his own palace and marry her himself; and, without even waiting for her consent to such an act, he gave orders for the marriage to take place that day and the rejoicings to begin at once.

The Princess of Bengal was awakened by the sound of drums beating, trumpets blowing, and all kinds of gay music, and wondered if it was some festival-day of Kashmir; but when, later, the sultan came to see her and said that these rejoicings were in honour of her marriage with himself, which he wished to take place that day, she was so overcome with surprise and dismay that she fainted away.

In alarm the sultan called the attendants to her aid, and they at length brought her round; and then the princess, rather than be married to the sultan, quickly thought of a clever plan to prevent such an act from taking place.

She pretended that she had suddenly gone mad, and began to shriek and to utter the wildest words, even rushing towards the sultan as though she meant to tear him in pieces.

The sultan was alarmed and grieved to see her in such a sad state of madness; and as she grew worse instead of better as the day went on, he was obliged to put off his marriage until the bride became more settled in her mind.

However, the princess kept up her pretended madness so well that at length the sultan sent for all the most learned doctors and cleverest wise men and wonder-workers in his kingdom, to see if they could cure her; but when the doctors were brought to the door of the princess's room, she only flew at them in the wildest rage, as though she would kill them, so that none dared to enter in; all indeed were glad to escape from such a dangerous person.

After some time had passed in this manner, and the doctors had even left off trying to cure the princess, and the sultan had begun to think he would have to give up all hope of ever marrying her, since he did not wish to have a mad wife, beautiful though she was, there came one day a poor dervish into the city, who, having taken up his abode at a khan or inn, began to enter into talk with the people gathered there.

This dervish was none other than Prince Firouz Schah of Persia, who had wandered through many countries in search of his lost princess, and happening, after great disappointment, to hear, in a certain city of India, of a Princess of Bengal who had gone suddenly mad on the very morn she was to have been married to the Sultan of Kashmir, he made fuller enquiries; and feeling sure that this must indeed be his own dear princess, he quickly made his way to the capital of Kashmir.

In the khan, where he stopped for rest and food, he heard from the idlers around the whole story of how the sultan had saved the Princess of Bengal from the wicked Hindu, whom he had caused to be beheaded. Glad to know that the base juggler was dead, he asked why the princess had not been returned to her father, or to the Prince of Persia, from whom she had been stolen.

He was told that the sultan, delighted with her beauty, had kept the princess, whom he had hoped to make his own bride, but that she had suddenly gone mad and had become so dangerous that the wedding had to be put off, and had not taken place yet; and although hundreds of the cleverest doctors in the kingdom had been called in, none of them could do anything to make her better.

The Prince of Persia, on hearing this, went out and got himself the robes of a doctor, which he put on; and then he made his way to the sultan's palace, where he told the attendants that he had come to cure the mad Princess of Bengal, for, though other doctors had failed, yet he knew that, by using a certain curious method known only to himself, he would succeed in bringing her back to her proper state of mind.

The attendants took this message to the sultan, who was

delighted to hear of a new doctor, none having come forward for a long time. He quickly took the disguised prince to a grated window in the palace, through which he could look into the room of the Princess of Bengal, without being seen by her, since she refused to allow strangers to approach her.

Prince Firouz Schah gazed eagerly through the grating, and, to his joy and relief, recognized in the mad lady, singing in the room beyond, his own lovely princess, whom he had sought so long and patiently; and he also noticed, by several signs, that her madness was only pretended, and guessed at once she was acting thus for his own sake, that she might remain true to him and prevent the Sultan of Kashmir from wishing to marry her.

The pretended doctor now told the sultan that he knew what was the cause of the princess's madness, and that he could certainly cure it, but he must first of all enter her room and speak with her alone, that he might know best how to deal with her; and so, after being warned to be on his guard, he was allowed to enter the room alone, and the door was shut behind him.

The princess, on seeing, as she supposed, a doctor at the door, at once rose up in a great rage and flew wildly at him; but when she came quite near, he said in a very low voice:

"Dear princess, I am not a doctor, but the Prince of Persia, and am here to save you from the sultan!"

The poor princess was so full of joy and surprise, on hearing this, that she could not speak at first; but Prince Firouz Schah quickly told her of his grief and wanderings in search of her, and begged to hear of her own adventures, that he might know better how to manage her escape.

After the princess had told her story, the prince asked if she knew what had become of the Enchanted Horse; and when she said that it had been kept in a safe place by the sultan, he soon thought out a clever plan to set her free.

They had been careful to talk in a low tone, and to act in a quiet manner, in case anyone might be watching them through the grated window; and having settled that the princess should appear rather better next day, and even receive the sultan more kindly, the pretended doctor left the room.

The sultan was quite delighted to learn that the princess was already a little better; and when he visited her next day, and found that she did not fly at him as before, but received him calmly, and even kindly, he declared on leaving the room that the new doctor was the cleverest man in the world and that all his directions must certainly be carried out.

The Prince of Persia, who was with him at the time, now asked how the Princess of Bengal came to be in Kashmir, as though he had never heard of the Enchanted Horse; and the sultan told him how he had saved her from a wicked Hindu who had brought her to his country on an Enchanted Horse, which he had since kept as a curiosity in a safe place, not knowing how to make use of it.

The pretended doctor now said that he felt sure some of the enchantment from the horse had entered into the princess, and was the cause of her madness, which could, however, be cured by a certain incense or powder of which he alone knew and some of which he had with him. He begged the sultan to have the Enchanted Horse brought out next day into the square before the palace gates, and the princess placed on its back, dressed in most gorgeous robes and jewels, and he would then work this wonderful cure before the whole court and people gathered round.

The sultan, doubting nothing, but glad to know that the princess could so soon be cured of her madness, when he would marry her at once, readily agreed to this request; and he gave orders that all things should be arranged just as the new doctor wished.

So next day the Enchanted Horse was brought out, and placed in the middle of the great square before the palace, where the sultan and his court, with crowds of the people, were gathered to watch the strange doctor work his wonderful cure; and presently the Princess of Bengal, most richly dressed, and almost covered with dazzling jewels, was led out of the palace, and set on the back of the magic steed.

Then fires were lighted all round her, and the pretended doctor, throwing some powder into each fire, solemnly ran three times round the horse, muttering what the people thought sure magic words.

The powder he had thrown into the fire-pots caused such a dense cloud of smoke to arise that the princess was quite hidden; and just at that moment the disguised prince sprang on to the back of the Enchanted Horse himself, and turned the peg. The horse instantly rose into the air with the two of them, the prince just having time to shout these words, which were quite plainly heard:

"Sultan of Kashmir, when next you wish to marry a princess who comes to you for protection and help learn first to obtain her consent!"

In a few moments the Enchanted Horse, bearing the Prince of Persia and the Princess of Bengal, vanished out of sight, and the Sultan of Kashmir was left to rail at himself for having been taken in by so simple a trick, and to swallow his disappointment as best he could.

The Enchanted Horse soon arrived in Persia; and in a very short time the prince and princess were married amidst great rejoicings, the King of Bengal being only too pleased to bestow his beautiful daughter on one who had gone through so much trouble and danger for her sake.

The Story of the Sisters

There was once a Sultan of Persia, named Khosrouschah, who was very fond of disguising himself and rambling through the city at night, in order to find out for himself if his subjects were satisfied with the manner in which he ruled them.

One evening, soon after he came to the throne, Khosrouschah went out on one of these rambles, taking with him his grand vizier, disguised like himself as a plain citizen, and, happening to hear voices as he passed by a certain house, he stopped to listen to what was being said.

The door was slightly ajar, and through the opening the sultan could see into a lighted room beyond, where three sisters were sitting chatting together after supper, and presently he gathered that wishes formed the subject of the talk.

"Well," said the eldest lady, "since we are talking of wishes, mine shall be to marry the sultan's chief baker, for then I should be able to eat as much as I pleased of those delicious cakes he makes, known as the sultan's bread."

"For my part," said the second sister, "I should like to be the wife of the sultan's chief cook, for then I should be able to enjoy the most dainty dishes and eat of the sultan's bread also, since, I am told, it is common enough in the palace."

It was now the turn of the youngest sister, who was very

beautiful indeed, and far more charming and clever than the other tvo, and she said: "What trifling wishes are yours, my sisters! For my part, I think there is no one to equal our lord and master, the sultan, and if my dearest wish could be granted, I should choose to be made the wife of Khosrouschah himself!"

The Sultan of Persia was so struck with the wishes of the three sisters, especially that of the youngest, whose beauty and charming manners delighted him, that he made up his mind to grant them their desires; and he commanded his grand vizier to remember the house, and to bring the ladies before him next morning. The grand vizier did so, and on the morrow he hurried the three sisters to the palace at once without telling them the reason, and scarcely giving them time to put on their best robes.

As soon as they had been brought before him, the sultan asked them if they remembered their wishes of the evening before, and when he saw that they were too much frightened and confused to reply, he said:

"Do not be afraid! I know what your wishes were, and I mean to grant them. You who wished to be my wife shall become so this very day; and you, "turning to the two elder sisters, "shall also have your wishes, and be married to my head cook and my chief baker!"

The youngest sister at once threw herself at the sultan's feet, pouring out her thanks, but declaring that she was not worthy of the great honour he would do her, and the two elder sisters also tried to excuse themselves. But the sultan would not be kept from his purpose, and the three weddings took place that same day.

The youngest sister's marriage was, of course, the most splendid, the rejoicings being as great as was usual at such a royal event; while those of the other sisters were celebrated just according to what was fitting to the position of a head cook and a chief baker.

Now, the two elder sisters, in spite of having had their wishes granted, soon began to feel the great difference between their youngest sister's dazzling rank and their own more lowly position; and at last they grew so madly jealous of the favoured young sultana, that they both made up their minds to do all they could to bring trouble upon her.

After making this wicked agreement, they had to wait patiently for some time before they could carry out their plans; but at last the chance came, and they were not slow to act. They had been careful to hide their dislike and jealousy from their sister, who still loved and trusted them as she had ever done, and so, when at length a baby prince was born to the young sultana, they came, so they said, to rejoice with her. But no sooner were the wicked sisters left alone with the sultana than they snatched up the baby prince, who was as fair as the day, and, carelessly wrapping him in a blanket, they put him in a basket, which they carried down to a little canal flowing beside the palace, where they left it to float away on the stream. They then obtained a little dead dog, and declared that this was the baby prince; and since they were the sisters of the sultana, and on that account not to be suspected of deceit, everyone believed them.

When he was told this disagreeable news the sultan was so angry and disappointed that he was ready to order his wife to be killed; but when the grand vizier pointed out how unjust such an act would be, he agreed to forgive her.

In the meanwhile, the basket in which the baby prince lay had been carried down the stream into the palace grounds, and here it was soon seen by the Governor of the Sultan's Gardens, one of the chief lords in the kingdom, who ordered a gardener to fetch it up on to the bank of the canal. The gardener did so, and when the basket was opened the baby was found inside.

Now, this governor had no children of his own, though he had always longed for them, so he carried the baby prince to his house, and desired his wife to bring him up as their son. His wife received the child with great joy, and showed him every loving care and attention, and the governor, though he suspected that the baby must have come from the palace, thought it best to keep the matter quiet at present, since it was not his business to interfere in other people's affairs.

Next year another little prince was born, and again the wicked sisters managed to seize the child and turn him adrift in a basket on the canal, showing to the sultan a dead cat, which they declared was the royal baby.

The sultan was again so angry that he would have destroyed the sultana had not the grand vizier persuaded him once more to have pity on her, and so the poor lady was allowed to live.

This second prince was also found by the governor of the Gardens, as he wandered through the palace grounds one morning, and without making further enquiries he took the child to his wife to be brought up as his own son.

As time went on a third child was born to the sultana, a princess, who met with the same treatment at the hands of the two wicked sisters; but, happily, this baby was also rescued from the canal by the Governor of the Garden, who took her to be cared for by his wife along with the two little princes, her brothers. Again the wicked sisters deceived the sultan, telling him that the sultana's child this time was but a piece of wood, which they showed him, and the sultan was now so enraged that he declared his wife to be a monster unfit to live, and ordered the grand vizier to have her put to death at once.

Again the good vizier persuaded his royal master to spare the sultana's life, but the sultan declared that it should only be on condition that she was kept as a prisoner and treated with great disrespect every day.

So, to the great joy of the two jealous sisters, the poor sultana, robed in the coarsest dress, was shut up in a wooden shed, with bars across the open window, built near the doors of the chief mosque, and the sultan gave orders that every person who went to the mosque to pray should be made to spit upon the unhappy prisoner, and show her every mark of disrespect.

In the meantime the Governor of the Gardens and his

wife brought up the two princes and the princess with as much loving care and kindness as though they were indeed their own children; and as the years went on they provided the very best masters and artists to teach them everything that it was fitting for them to know. They named the two princes, Bahman and Perviz, and the princess, Parizade, all of which were favourite royal names in Persia. The two young princes were very handsome, and so clever that they soon learnt all that the wisest masters could teach them, and were wonderfully skilful in every princely exercise and art; and the princess was in no way behind her brothers, for, besides being beautiful, amiable, and charming, she was also surprisingly witty and clever.

The Governor of the Gardens was delighted with the cleverness and truly royal bearing of his adopted children, and as soon as they had grown out of childhood, and were finished with their studies, he determined to find a more suitable abode for them than his plain house near the palace gates. He ordered a magnificent house to be built in the midst of a beautiful park he had bought, which lay at a short distance from the city, and when it was finished he furnished it in the most splendid style, and surrounded it with delightful gardens. He then begged the sultan to allow him to retire from court, since he was now growing old; and, having taken leave of his royal master, he went with his adopted children to the beautiful country house he had just built. His wife was already dead, and he had not enjoyed his new home for long when he himself was seized by a sudden illness, which ended in his death.

The two princes and their sister mourned deeply for the good Governor, whom they had always believed to be their father, and, as his last illness had so suddenly ended in death that he had not had time to tell them anything of the manner in which he had found them, they still had no idea of their royal birth. They had a large enough fortune for all their wants, and as they loved one another dearly they continued to live together very happily in the beautiful home that had been built for them.

One day, when the two young princes had gone out hunting, and the Princess Parizade had remained at home, an old religious woman came to the gates, and begged to be allowed to say her prayers in the little oratory, or prayingplace, that had been built in the house. The princess granted her leave to do so, and ordered the servants to show the good old woman all over the house and the gardens when she had prayed as long as she wished.

So, when the holy woman had finished saying her prayers, the attendants took her to view the beautiful house and grounds which the Governor of the Sultan's Gardens had been at such trouble and expense to provide for his adopted children; and, after she had seen and admired everything, they led her into the presence of the princess, who received her very kindly, and invited her to refresh herself with some fine fruits and dainty cakes that she had ordered to be set out for her.

Whilst the religious woman was eating, the princess sat beside her, and talked with her about the holy life of prayer which she led; but presently she changed the subject, and asked her guest what she thought about the house and grounds she had just seen, and whether she liked them.

"Madam, "replied the holy woman, "the gardens are beautiful and the house is magnificent, and it seems to me that there are but three things wanting to make your home the most perfect in the world."

Full of curiosity, the Princess Parizade begged to be told what these three things were, and the old woman said:

"Madam, the first is the Speaking Bird, which has the wonderful power of drawing around it all the singing birds in the neighbourhood, which come to join in its ever-joyful song; the second is the Singing Tree, the leaves of which are mouths, and form a delightful, never-ending concert of different voices; and the third is the Yellow Water, a single bright golden drop of which, if poured into a basin, increases so quickly as to fill it instantly, and rises up in the middle like a fountain, which constantly plays, yet does not overflow the basin."

"Oh, how wonderful are these things, good mother! "cried the princess. "And how grateful I am to you for telling me of them! I beg of you to satisfy me still further by saying where they are to be found, that I may try to get them!"

"Madam," replied the religious woman, "you have treated me so kindly that I will tell you. They are all to be met with in the same spot, on the border of this country, towards India. Anyone you may send for these treasures must take the road that lies before your house, and follow it for twenty days; and on the twentieth, if he asks the first person he then meets where the Speaking Bird, the Singing Tree, and the Yellow Water are to be found, he will be told." So saying, the religious woman took leave of the princess, and went on her way.

The Princess Parizade was so much struck with the thought of the three wonderful curiosities of which she had just been told, that she felt she should never be satisfied until she had obtained them, although she feared there might be many difficulties in the way. After the old woman had gone, she sat lost in thought until her brothers returned from hunting. The two young princes were surprised to find their usually gay sister so quiet and thoughtful, and begged to know the reason of it. After a little coaxing, the Princess Parizade told them of the religious woman's visit, and of the three things she had declared were wanting to make their home perfect.

"And now, my brothers," added the princess, "please tell me what person you think I should send for these curiosities, which I now feel are really necessary for our future happiness and delight, and without which I shall never be satisfied."

The two princes were greatly struck with their sister's story, and agreed with her that, having been told of such wonderful treasures, they ought certainly to try to obtain them; and, since both of them had a great love of adventure, they declared that they would undertake the search themselves.

However, as they did not care to leave their sister alone, it was agreed that the eldest brother, Prince Bahman, should make the first journey, whilst Prince Perviz remained at home to attend to matters there. The rest of the evening was spent in arranging their plans, and in going over all that the religious woman had said.

Early next morning Prince Bahman mounted his horse, ready to start on his journey; but, just as he was bidding farewell to his brother and sister, the Princess Parizade cried: "Alas, my brother! I had forgotten that you may meet with dangers on the way, and I may never see you again ! Pray, do not go; for, rather than that harm should happen to you, I would give up all hope of securing the Speaking Bird, the Singing Tree, and the Yellow Water, wonderful treasures though they be!"

"Sister, "replied the Prince Bahman, smiling at the sudden alarm of Princess Parizade, "I am determined to go. The dangers of which you speak happen only to the unlucky. It is true that I may be among that number, but I may also be among the successful, and there are far more successful people than unsuccessful. Since I may fail, accept this knife, my sister, and look at it sometimes. Whenever you see it clean and bright, as it is now, you will know that I am alive and well; but if it becomes dull and stained with blood, it will be a sure sign that I am dead !"

Having said these words, Prince Bahman again bade his sister and brother farewell, and rode away. He took the road that lay in front of the house, and journeyed straight ahead, without turning to the right or to the left.

On the twentieth day he met with a frightful-looking old man, who was sitting beneath a tree on the roadside, not very far from a small thatched house, which was evidently his home. His hair was as white as snow, and his beard hung down to his feet; the nails of his hands and feet had grown long like claws; and, for clothes, he wore an old mat round his body, and a broad flat hat like an umbrella on his head.

This hideous-looking old man was a dervish, who, having given himself up to a holy life of prayer, had lived in this lonely place away from the stir of life for a great many years; and Prince Bahman, remembering that he was to ask directions from the first person he met, went up to the holy man and bade him good-day.

The dervish replied to him; but the prince could scarcely hear the words he said, owing to the thick whiskers which hung over the old man's mouth. As he did not mean to go without the directions he needed, Prince Bahman tied his horse to a tree, and, pulling out a pair of scissors he had with him, he went up to the old man, and said:

"Good dervish, I want to speak with you, but your whiskers keep me from hearing what you say. Pray, let me cut some of them off, for indeed you look more like a bear than a man."

The dervish did not seem to object, so Prince Bahman cut off as much hair as he thought necessary, and when he had finished he declared that the dervish now looked quite young and pleasant-looking. The dervish was so pleased with this compliment that he said he should be glad to do anything he could for the young man in return for his trouble, and Prince Bahman at once said: "Then, please, good father, tell me where the Speaking Bird, the Singing Tree, and the Yellow Water are to be found. I am searching for these treasures, and shall be glad if you can show me the way."

On hearing this, the dervish seemed troubled, and did not reply for some time; but at last he said: "The road you ask for is well known to me, but, since I love you so much, I hesitate to grant your request, for there is much danger in the journey you would undertake, and you are almost certain to lose your life if you persist in going. I have directed many other young adventurers to the place where the treasures are to be found; but they have all died, and no one has ever returned! Therefore, let me advise you to give up your search, and go back home."

However, Prince Bahman was not to be kept from his purpose by these alarming words; and, seeing that nothing he could say would make him turn back, the dervish sighed deeply, and taking a bowl out of a bag beside him, placed it in his hands, saying:

"Since you will not listen to my advice, take this bowl, and, when you have mounted your horse, throw it before you. It will begin to roll at a great rate, and you must follow it to the foot of a certain mountain, where it will stop. You must climb this mountain, and as you mount higher and higher you will notice a great many large black stones on every side, and will hear a terrible din of voices calling you bad names, and shouting out all kinds of rude remarks to make you turn back. However, do not let these magic voices of invisible persons frighten you, and, above all things, do not look behind you, for, if you do, at that very instant you will be changed into a black stone like the others around you, for these were all once brave young men like yourself, who failed to follow my directions. If you escape this danger, go on to the top of the mountain, where you will see a cage, in which is the Speaking Bird you seek; and if you ask him where the Singing Tree and the Yellow Water are to be found, he will tell you! That is all I have to say, you know what you have to do and what to avoid. If you trust me you will follow the direction which I have given you, and not risk your life."

Prince Bahman took the bowl, and, thanking the dervish for his advice and directions, he mounted his horse and went on his way. He threw the bowl before him, and it rolled on in front at such a great rate that it was all he could do to keep it in sight. At length, however, it came to the foot of a huge gloomy mountain, where it stopped; and Prince Bahman now found that the dangers and terrors the dervish had told him of were very real indeed.

As he began to climb the mountain he trembled when on

every side of him he saw great black stones in the shape of men and horses, and he had scarcely gone a few steps before he heard dreadful voices shouting to him, though no one was in sight. Some of the voices called him "thief", "murderer", and other bad names; and others shrieked out rude, mocking remarks into his ears, as though to anger him and prevent him from going forward.

For some time Prince Bahman went steadily on, without looking behind him, trying not to be alarmed by the evil sounds around him; but, as he mounted higher, the dreadful shrieking voices got worse and worse, and at last he grew so terrified that, forgetting the dervish's directions, he turned round, meaning to run down the hill again. At that very instant he was changed into a black stone like the others around him; and his horse also underwent the same fate.

In the meantime Princess Parizade and Prince Perviz were impatiently awaiting their brother's return; and every day since Prince Bahman had left, the Princess took out the knife he had given her, to learn whether he was still alive and well. On the evening of the day on which Prince Bahman had been turned into a black stone she took out the knife as usual, to look at in the presence of Prince Perviz; and, to the horror of both, they saw that the blade was now stained with blood, and knew at once that their brother was dead.

For a long while they were too much overcome with grief to speak; but at last Prince Perviz declared that, since his brother was dead, it was useless to waste time in mourning, and knowing that the princess still desired above all things to have the treasures of which the religious woman had told her, he said he should now undertake to search for them himself.

The Princess Parizade did all she could to persuade him not to go, since she did not wish to lose both her brothers; but nothing that she could say would keep him from his purpose. He then gave her a string of a hundred pearls, and told her that if they would not run on the string when she counted them, but remained fixed, she would know that he was dead; but so long as the pearls remained loose, it was a sign that he was alive and well.

Earty next morning he mounted his horse and set off on his journey, taking the same road as his brother had done. On the twentieth day he met with the same dervish; and going up to him at once, he asked if he could tell him where to look for the Speaking Bird, the Singing Tree, and the Yellow Water.

The dervish tried to persuade him not to go farther, telling him that he would certainly meet with the same sad fate as another young man who had come to him lately for these very directions, and who had been changed into a black stone in attempting to carry them out.

But, although Prince Perviz knew that the young man mentioned must have been his own brother, Bahman, he said he still hoped to meet with better success himself; and then, finding that he was not to be kept from his purpose, the dervish told him to take a bowl out of a bag nearby, which would show him the way. He also gave him the same directions and warnings as he had given to Prince Bahman; and after thanking the old man for his gift and advice, Prince Perviz again mounted his horse, and, throwing the bowl in front of him, he followed it until it stopped at the foot of the mountain.

Not giving himself time to be alarmed or turned from his purpose at the warning sight of the great black stones he saw on every side, he began to climb the mountain at once; but scarcely had he gone half a dozen steps when he heard a loud, angry voice from just behind shout in his ear: "Stop, foolish youth, that I may punish you for daring to come here!"

Prince Perviz was so angry at being addressed in such an insulting tone that he drew his sword, and, forgetting what the dervish had said, turned round to strike the speaker, who was, of course, invisible; but at that same instant, before he had time to move another step, he and his horse were changed into black stones.

Now it happened that the Princess Parizade at that same

moment was counting the string of pearls Prince Perviz had given her before he left, and to her dismay, as she was passing the pearls over the string as usual, they suddenly became fixed and would not move, a sure sign that her brother was dead.

Although full of grief at having thus lost both her brothers, the princess would not despair, nor waste her time in useless weeping; and since there was now nothing to keep her at home, she quickly made up her mind to undertake the same wild journey herself, to learn for certain the fate of the two young princes, and to seek for the treasures she still longed to possess. So, next morning, she dressed herself in man's clothing, and mounted her horse; and having told her servants that she hoped to return in a few days, she set off, taking the same road she had seen her brothers take. On the twentieth day she met with the same old dervish; and, alighting from her horse, she went and sat down beside him, saying as she did so: "Pray let me rest beside you for a while, good dervish; and please tell me, if you can, where I shall find the Speaking Bird, the Singing Tree, and the Yellow Water."

For a long while the dervish, who knew her to be a lady in spite of her man's dress, would not tell her anything about the means of reaching these treasures, and did all he could to persuade her to return home; but seeing that she would not listen to such advice, he began to describe to her all the dangers and difficulties with which she would meet if she persisted in her purpose, taking care to exaggerate all the details in order to make her lose courage.

When the dervish had finished speaking the princess said:

"You do not frighten me, good dervish, and I hope still to succeed in spite of what you say. I shall certainly remember not to turn round when climbing the mountain, no matter what sounds I may hear behind me; and as for the dreadful voices, I have just thought of a fine plan which will lessen that terror for me. I shall stop up both my ears with cotton, which will prevent me from hearing the dreadful sounds quite so plainly; and by this means I shall hope to be able to keep my wits about me, and to reach the top of the mountain in safety."

The dervish declared that he had never heard of any former adventurers making use of such a simple means of avoiding the chief terror of the mountain; and, although he still begged the princess not to venture farther, he now placed a bowl in her hands, and gave her the same directions as he had given to the young princes.

The princess thanked the dervish and quickly mounted her horse; then, throwing the bowl straight in front of her, she followed it until it stopped at the bottom of the mountain. Here she alighted from her horse, and gazed sadly at the many black stones that met her view; and then, stopping up her ears with some cotton she had with her, she began to climb the mountain. She could hear the angry voices, but they sounded a long way off; and although they grew louder and wilder the higher she mounted, the cotton she had put in her ears prevented the full terror of the sounds from reaching her. She heard many rude, mocking speeches, but only laughed at them, and in spite of all the shrieks, commands, and horrible din of voices, she did not once look behind her.

At last she got close to the mountain-top, where she could see the cage and the Speaking Bird, which screamed out louder than any of the other voices, and bade her go back at once.

But the Princess Parizade took no more notice of his voice than she had done of the other sounds, and, bravely climbing to the very summit of the rocks, she boldly seized the cage in her hands, and cried out: "Now, Bird, I have got you safe at last, in spite of your tricks! You shall not escape!"

Since the voices had now ceased, the princess pulled the cotton out of her ears; and as she did so the Speaking Bird said:

"Brave lady, pray do not be angry with me for the terrors with which I have plagued you; for now that you have succeeded in taking me from the rock, I have become your slave! I know who you really are, although you do not yourself, and the time will come when I shall be able to serve you in such a way as to bring great happiness upon you. And now, to prove that I am indeed your faithful slave, pray command me, and you shall see that I am ready to obey you!"

The princess was delighted when she heard these words; and she said:

"Bird, I am glad that you bear such good will towards me. Pray tell me where I shall find the wonderful Yellow Water of which I have been told!"

The bird at once pointed out the place to her; and as it was close by, the princess went up to the Yellow Water and filled a little silver jug she had brought with her for the purpose.

She then came back to the Speaking Bird, and asked him to tell her where she should find the Singing Tree and the bird told her to go into a wood just behind her where she would find what she sought. The princess went into the wood, and soon found the Singing Tree by the delightful concert of sweet music made by its leaves; but as it was too large for her to think of pulling it up by the roots and carrying it home, she had to come back again to the bird and ask his advice as to what she should do. The bird told her that a little branch of the Singing Tree was quite enough for her to take, for if she planted even a twig of it in her garden it would soon grow into as fine a tree as the one she had seen. So the princess went back to the wood and broke off a branch of the Singing Tree; and then she returned to the Speaking Bird, and said:

"Bird, I am not yet satisfied ! You have been the cause of my two brothers' deaths, and I know they are amongst the black stones on this mountain. Tell me how to restore them to their natural forms again, that I may take them home with me."

At first the Speaking Bird would not reply, but at last he said: "You ask me a difficult thing, yet I am ready to do it for you. If you will look around you will see a little pitcher. Take it, and sprinkle a few drops of the water that is in it upon every black stone. They will at once take on their proper forms again; and this is the only way in which you will be able to find your brothers. Do not fear that you will be changed into stone yourself as you go down the mountain, for since you have taken me from my rock you have conquered the magic of this place."

The princess soon found the pitcher of water. and, taking it up, together with the cage, the jug of Yellow Water, and the branch of the Singing Tree, she began to walk down the mountain, and, as she went, poured a little of the magic water from the pitcher upon every black stone, which instantly was changed into a man. She was careful not to miss out even one, so that all the stone figures of men and horses took on their own natural forms again; and presently, to her great joy, she saw her two brothers coming towards her from amidst the joyful crowd.

The two princes ran to embrace their sister, astonished to find her there; and in answer to her questions as to what they were doing on the mountains, they replied that they had been asleep.

"Yes," cried the Princess Parizade, "and you might have slept for ever had it not been for me." She then told them of her own adventures upon the mountains, and how she had succeeded in obtaining the Speaking Bird and other treasures of which the religious woman had told her, and how she had restored all the black stones to their natural shapes.

Prince Bahman and Prince Perviz gratefully thanked their sister over and over again for having been ready to brave such dangers for their sakes; and all the other gentlemen, who had crowded round to hear her story, declared that, so far from envying her for the treasures she had got, and which they had failed to obtain, they felt that the least they could do to show their thankfulness to her for having restored them to life was to offer themselves as her slaves.

But the Princess Parizade would not hear of this, and declared that everyone was free to return to his own home, since it was sufficient reward for her to have her dear brothers alive once more; and then, as there was no further need for them to stay upon the mountain, she proposed that they should all mount their horses and ride away.

The princes and gentlemen were ready enough to do so, and they insisted that the princess herself should be their leader; so when all the company had mounted their horses they left the gloomy mountain behind them with great joy, and rode off at once, the Princess Parizade leading the way. They stopped when they came to the hut of the dervish, meaning to thank him for the good and true advice he had given them, but they found to their surprise that the old man was dead, whether of old age, or because he was no longer needed to point out the way to the treasures found by the princess, they could not tell.

They went on with their journey, their numbers growing less each day as the gentlemen came to the various roads that led to their own particular homes; and at last the two princes and the princess were left to ride alone until they, too, reached the beautiful home they loved so well, and which they had never expected to see again.

After the wanderers had been received with great joy by their servants, the Princess Parizade placed the cage containing the precious Speaking Bird in the garden; and no sooner did the bird begin to sing than he drew around him all the larks, nightingales, and other singing birds in the neighbourhood to join in his joyous song. She next took the branch of the Singing Tree, and planted it in one of the flower-beds, where it at once took root, and soon grew into a large tree, the leaves of which were mouths, and gave out as delightful a concert of sweet voices as those of the tree from which it had been taken.

After this was done, the Princess ordered a huge basin of most beautiful marble to be set up in the middle of the garden; and when it was ready, she poured into it the Yellow Water from the little jug, which at once increased until it filled the basin and rose up into a fountain twenty feet high, which though it constantly played, yet it never overflowed the basin.

The news of these great wonders quickly spread all over the country-side, and as the gates of the house and gardens were shut to no one, people came from all parts to admire them.

One day, soon after their return, Prince Bahman and Prince Perviz went out hunting, which was their favourite pastime; but instead of hunting in their own park as usual, they rode farther, to seek game on land at a considerable distance from their house.

Whilst they were enjoying their sport, it happened that the Sultan of Persia came to hunt upon the same ground. The two young princes were about to leave the park, out of respect for the royal hunter, when, instead of avoiding him, as they had wished to do, they suddenly came face to face with him in a narrow place. At once they sprang from their horses, and bowed low before him. The sultan was so struck with their handsome looks and respectful behaviour that he asked who they were and where they lived.

Prince Bahman replied that they were the sons of the late Governor of the Royal Gardens, and that they lived in a house which he had built for them just before his death; and then the sultan, having learnt that they were fond of hunting, invited them to join him in the hunt that was about to begin.

The two princes gladly accepted the invitation, and the sultan was more charmed than ever when he saw how skilful and fearless they were in the chase; for they each tracked out and killed a lion and a bear in a wonderfully short time, and were about to make another dangerous attack, when the sultan sent for them to come to talk to him. When they came before him he admired their skill and bravery, and was delighted with their modest manners and noble bearing in his presence; and, already feeling a great love for the two handsome youths, he presently invited them to pay him a visit at his palace.

At first the young princes begged to be excused. Upon the sultan asking for their reason, Prince Bahman explained that they had a sister at home whom they loved so dearly that they never accepted an invitation without first consulting her wishes.

The sultan praised them for their brotherly conduct, and

asked them to consult their sister and to bring him an answer next day, when he arranged to meet them in the same place. Soon afterwards the two princes returned home.

They did not, however, remember to speak of their meeting with the royal hunter nor of his invitation. So, when they met the sultan next day, they were obliged to confess to him that they had forgotten to mention the matter to their sister. But the sultan very kindly forgave them.

They even forgot to do so a second time, and again the sultan kindly forgave them; but on this occasion he put into Prince Bahman's vest three little golden balls, which would remind him of his promise when they rolled out as he undressed himself, if he did not remember before.

The two princes would have again forgotten their message had it not been for the golden balls, which rolled on to the floor as Prince Bahman unfastened his robe at night; and suddenly remembering the sultan's invitation, they hurried to their sister's room, and, finding that she not yet retired to rest, they entered and told her of their meeting with the sultan, and of his wish that they would visit him.

The Princess Parizade was by no means pleased with this news; for she felt that if her brothers visited the sultan, he would soon persuade them to enter his service, and then she would lose them as her own companions, and be obliged to live a lonely life by herself. But she said that, before they decided one way or the other, she would ask the advice of the Speaking Bird, who was wonderfully wise, and had promised to help her in every difficult matter. So she sent for the cage; and when it had been brought, she told the Speaking Bird of the sultan's invitation, and asked him to say what her brothers should do in this matter.

To her surprise the Bird at once answered:

"Your brothers must do as the sultan wishes, and also ask him to visit your house in return."

"But, bird, I shall lose my beloved brothers if the sultan takes a fancy to them," said the princess.

"Not at all," replied the Bird, "You will still be happy together; but you must certainly invite the sultan to come here. Take my advice, and all will be well."

After this the princess said nothing more; and next morning, when the two princes met the sultan, they told him that their sister was willing for them to accept his invitation. The sultan was delighted to hear this; and, after a short hunt, he rode back to the palace, taking the two princes with him.

As they entered the capital, all the people turned to look at the noble young strangers riding on either side of the sultan; and many wished that their royal master had been blessed with two such handsome princes to reign after him.

On arriving at the palace a splendid feast was served, and whilst they refreshed themselves the sultan talked to the two princes, and was more delighted than ever with the clever remarks they made and with the ease with which they talked on every subject. He was astonished that his late Governor of the Gardens should have had such noble children, and many times that evening he wished that he himself had been blessed with two such handsome, accomplished sons.

As the evening went on a delightful concert and entertainment took place, and when this came to an end the two princes rose to take leave of the sultan, thanking him for the kindness that he had shown to them. The sultan begged that they would come often to see him, and they promised to do so, and before leaving the room Prince Bahman, saying that their sister would be delighted to receive him, humbly invited the sultan to honour them with a visit to their own home when next he came hunting that way. The sultan was so pleased with this invitation that he said he would come on the very next day. He desired the two princes to meet him in the same place where he had seen them on the first occasion and to act as his guides.

When the princes returned home they told their sister of the royal visit she was to receive on the next day, and as soon as she was left alone the princess asked the Speaking Bird to tell her how she must entertain the sultan so as to please him in every way. The bird told her to order her cooks to prepare as good a feast as they could. "And", he added, "be sure you tell them to make ready a dish of cucumbers stuffed with pearls, which must be set before the sultan directly the feast begins!"

The princess was amazed at being told to provide such an unheard-of dish as cucumbers stuffed with pearls, and she declared that all the pearls she possessed would not be enough for so extravagant a purpose. But the bird said:

"Mistress, do as I tell you and all will be well. If you have not enough pearls for the dish of which I tell you, go tomorrow morning and dig beneath the first tree on your right hand in the park, and there you will find plenty."

Early next morning Princess Parizade called a gardener to attend her, and, leading him to the tree of which the bird had told her, she bade him dig into the ground at the foot of it. The gardener did so, and after digging for some time he found a gold box, which he gave to his mistress. The princess opened the box, and finding it to be full of pearls she returned with it to the house, and showing it to her brothers she told them what the Speaking Bird had advised her to do with them. The princes were as much surprised as herself at the strange dish the bird advised them to place before the sultan, but they all agreed that they would do well to follow out his directions. So the princess sent for her chief cook, and giving him the box of pearls ordered him to use them to stuff a dish of cucumbers he was to prepare for the feast that evening; and the cook, though greatly astonished, took the pearls, and said he would prepare the dish himself.

At the time agreed upon the two princes went to meet the sultan, and after hunting for a while they led him to their house, where their sister was ready to receive them.

The sultan was so much charmed with the beauty and graceful manners of Princess Parizade that he declared he was not surprised that her brothers were unwilling to leave her for even a short time, and after a little talk with her he begged that she would be his guide through the house and the grounds, which he had been told contained such wonderful treasures. Princess Parizade gladly agreed to do so, and as she led the way the sultan was more struck than ever with her beauty and royal bearing.

The princess showed the sultan all over the house, and after he had admired everything, and expressed his astonishment at all he had seen, she led him into the gardens. Here the first object that met his eyes was the wonderful golden fountain of Yellow Water, and when the princess explained to him how the fountain had been formed from one small jug of the water, he was utterly amazed. He was even more surprised when presently the princess led him to the Singing Tree, and he heard the delightful concert of sweet voices that came from its leaves. He begged her to tell him how she had come to possess wonders such as he had never even heard of before. The princess replied that the story of the Singing Tree and the Yellow Water was closely connected with that of a Speaking Bird, which she would next show him; and she promised to tell him this story as soon as he had rested and refreshed himself.

She then led him into the great hall where the feast was to be served, and as they drew near the sultan was surprised to notice that hundreds of birds crowded the trees close to the open window of the hall, where the princess pointed out to him the Speaking Bird in his cage. She explained the power which the bird had of attracting all the other singing birds in the neighbourhood around him, and then she said to the Speaking Bird: "My slave, the sultan is here!"

"The sultan is welcome," said the Speaking Bird. "Long may he live!"

The sultan thanked the bird for his welcome, and then he sat down to the splendid feast that had been prepared for him. The dish of cucumbers was at once set before him, and he was so astonished when he found that they were stuffed with pearls that he turned to the princess and the two princes, and said: "What strange dish is this? Why are these cucumbers stuffed with pearls which cannot be eaten?"

Before anyone else could reply, the Speaking Bird said:

"Can Your Majesty be so surprised at being served with cucumbers stuffed with pearls, which you can see plainly for yourself, and yet believe that the sultana your wife had for children a dog, a cat, and a piece of wood?"

"I believe that," replied the sultan, "because two ladies whom I trusted told me it was the truth!"

"You were deceived!" said the Speaking Bird; and he then told the sultan the whole story of how the sultana's wicked sisters had cast away the royal children, and how they had been found and brought up by the Governor of his Gardens.

When the sultan understood that the two handsome youths and the beautiful maiden before him were indeed his own children, he was overjoyed; and after embracing them many times, and talking again with them, he said: "Tomorrow, my dear children, I shall bring the sultana, your mother, to see you!"

When the feast was over the sultan returned to the palace, and the very first thing he did on his arrival was to order the sultana's two wicked sisters to be seized and executed at once. When this had been done he went with his lords and attendants to the door of the great mosque, and took the poor sultana out of the prison-cage, where she had spent so many wretched years. After begging her to forgive him for his harsh treatment of her, he embraced her many times, and, telling her the story of his meeting with their three children, he said they would visit them together on the morrow.

So the sultana was restored to her former rank, to the great joy of all the people, who had always loved her, and next day she was clad in magnificent robes and went with the sultan and his whole Court to the house built by the Governor of the Gardens.

As soon as they arrived the sultan presented the two princes and the princess to the sultana, who embraced them again and again, and was overjoyed to find that her children had grown up to be so handsome, clever, and charming.

A splendid feast had been prepared for the royal guests,

and when this had been enjoyed, the sultan and his children led the sultana into the gardens, and showed her its many beauties, and also the wonderful treasures, to obtain which the Princess Parizade had been through such dangers. Later in the day the royal party returned to the capital, the sultan riding with Prince Bahman and Prince Perviz on his right hand, and the sultana and Princess Parizade on the left; and as they rode through the streets, attended by their dazzling Court, crowds of people followed them, shouting and singing with joy as they welcomed the royal children. The princess carried the Speaking Bird in her hand, and as he sang, his sweet notes attracted all the other singing birds, which followed him in flocks, flying from tree to tree, and from house-top to house-top. In this joyous manner the royal party arrived at the palace, where rejoicings and merrymakings were held for many days.

Aladdin and the Wonderful Lamp

There once lived, in a certain large city of China, a poor tailor named Mustapha, who was so very badly off that, though he worked hard all day, it was as much as he could do to keep himself and his household from starving. To make matters worse, his only child, a boy named Aladdin, had been brought up so badly, and was so lazy, careless, and disobedient that, instead of being a help and comfort to his parents, he was only a trouble to them. He was really a clever boy, but instead of learning all the wise and useful things he could, he chose to play about in the streets with other idle children. Even when he grew older, and was put to learn his father's trade, he still refused to work, and, directly he was left to himself, he would run away to join his wicked companions for the rest of the day.

At last the poor tailor, quite overcome by his own misfortunes, and grieved at his son's bad conduct, became very ill, and died. The mother, finding that Aladdin did not mean to work at his father's trade, sold up the things in the shop, and tried to earn a wretched living by spinning cotton.

Aladdin still went on with his idle, careless ways until he was almost grown-up, and then a strange thing happened, which changed the whole course of his life for the better.

One day a stranger, who was really a wicked sorcerer, or wizard, known as the African magician, passed through the city, and saw Aladdin at play with some of his idle companions. Noticing at once that the lad was really quick and clever, he made up his mind to make use of him in carrying out some secret plan which he had on hand.

So, after learning what he could about him from the bystanders, he called Aladdin to one side, and asked him if he was the son of Mustapha, the tailor.

Aladdin replied that he was, but that his father had been dead a long time; and then, to his surprise, the stranger threw his arms round his neck and kissed him many times, weeping as he did so. On being asked by Aladdin why he acted thus, the African magician told him that he was his uncle, and that he wept for the death of Mustapha, the tailor, who was his brother. He then gave Aladdin a handful of small money, and told him to go back to his mother, and tell her that his newly-found uncle would visit her the next day.

Full of surprise and delight, Aladdin ran off home at once, and asked his mother if he had an uncle. The poor woman replied that he had not, and when Aladdin told her about the stranger who had just spoken to him, she decided there must be some mistake, for though her husband had certainly had a brother once upon a time, he had long since been dead.

But next day Aladdin again met with the African magician, who kissed him as before, and, putting two gold pieces into his hand, told him to take them to his mother, and bid her get a good supper ready, as he meant to come and see her that night without fail.

He made the lad show him the house where he lived, and then went away.

In great excitement Aladdin ran to his mother, and, giving her the two gold pieces, told her what the stranger had said; and this time she got ready a supper for her expected visitor, greatly wondering who he could really be.

When evening came, the African magician arrived, bringing wines and rich fruits with him for the supper; and when they were all seated at the little feast, he told Aladdin's mother that he was indeed her husband's longlost brother, whom all had believed to be dead, and that for forty years he had been travelling about in various parts of the world, until at last he had such a longing to see his brother Mustapha once again that he had returned to China only to be met with the news of his death.

Now, all this was really only a wicked story, but the cunning magician wept so bitterly when he spoke of his brother's death, and declared that he felt so much love for Aladdin, because of his exact likeness to his father, that the poor widow woman began to believe that he spoke the truth; and as for Aladdin, he was quite ready to accept for his uncle a stranger who treated him so kindly and seemed so rich and powerful.

So when the magician said that he meant to provide for Aladdin and start him in life as a rich merchant, the mother w as very willing that he should do so, hoping that her idle son would now turn from his bad ways and be a comfort to her. Aladdin, though he had always hated work, was delighted at the idea of so easily becoming a rich and powerful merchant.

And now the magician, having made such a good beginning, felt well pleased with himself, and soon hoped to make use of Aladdin for his own wicked purposes. On the very next day he took the boy out with him into the city, first of all buying him a handsome suit of clothes, and then taking him to all the places where the richest merchants met together. He invited many of them to a grand supper at night, which he gave in honour of his pretended nephew.

Aladdin was full of delight at the happy prospect now before him, and when the magician came again for him next day, saying that he must now visit the many splendid gardens and palaces on the borders of the city, he was only too eager to go. He gaily bid his mother farewell little dreaming of the dreadful adventure that would befall him ere he saw her again.

The wicked magician did not mean that the poor widow woman should ever see her son again, for that very day he determined to carry out the plan he had formed, and for which he wished to make use of Aladdin.

So he took the boy to the borders of the city, where the richest people lived in fine houses and palaces set in the midst of most beautiful large gardens; and by constantly telling him of finer sights yet to come, he artfully led him through garden after garden until they were a great way from the city.

When they began to feel hungry and tired, the magician suggested that they should rest by a fountain in one of the gardens, and, drawing out a handkerchief full of cakes and fruits which he had brought with him, he spread it out for a meal, and while they ate he talked very kindly to Aladdin, advising him to give up his idle ways and bad companions and to seek wise friends and useful knowledge, since he would soon be a man, and have to make a name for himself.

When the meal was over they went on with their walk, leaving the gardens behind them, and going far out into the country, in search of the most beautiful garden of all, so the cunning magician said.

Aladdin had never been so far before, and he did not like the looks of the high mountains and the lonely country through which they were now treading, but the false uncle told him many interesting stories to prevent him from noticing where he was going and from feeling too tired.

At last they came to a narrow valley between two mountains, and here they stopped, the magician saying they would go no farther, for he would now show Aladdin something very wonderful. He first of all bade the boy gather together some dry sticks in a heap for a fire, and then, when this was done, he made a great blaze, and throwing into the midst of it some incense-powder, which caused a dense smoke to arise, he uttered several magical words.

Instantly the ground opened just in front of the magician, showing a large flat stone, with a brass ring fixed in the middle of it.

Aladdin was so surprised and terrified at this magic that

he tried to run away; but his pretended uncle seized hold of him, and, with scolding words, gave him such a rough box on the ears that he fell to the ground. The poor lad got up again with tears in his eyes, and asked his uncle what he had done to deserve such treatment.

The magician now spoke gently to him again, saying that he must certainly obey him as his uncle if he wished to obtain the good things in store for him. He then told Aladdin that beneath the stone before them there was hidden a great treasure, which would be his alone if he would obey him. He also said that Aladdin was the only person in the world who was permitted to lift the stone, and that, if he would seize hold of the brass ring, and at the same time utter the names of his father and his grandfather, he would be able to raise it quite easily.

Aladdin, having now got over his fright, and being full of curiosity, did exactly as his uncle told him; and when he had pulled up the stone he saw beneath it a hollow space a few feet deep, with a small door, and steps leading down into the ground.

"And now, my son," said the magician, "listen to what I have to say. Go down those steps, and through an open door, which leads into three great halls, in each of which you will find four large brass vases on either side filled with gold and silver. Be sure you do not meddle with these; and, above all things, do not touch the walls, even with your clothes, or you will die instantly! Go straight forward without stopping, and at the end of the third hall you will find another door leading into a garden planted with most beautiful fruit-trees. Walk along the garden path until you come to five steps, at the top of which you will see a niche that holds a lighted lamp.

"Take down the lamp, put out the light, pour away the liquid within it, and then bring it to me. Do what I desire you at once; but if you wish for any of the fruit in the garden you may gather as much as you like!"

As he said these words the magician took a ring from his

pocket, and put it on Aladdin's finger, saying it would protect him from evil so long as he did as he had just been bidden. He again told him to go boldly down the steps, and to bring back treasures that would make them both rich for life.

Aladdin was quite ready to obey, and, jumping into the little cave, he went down the steps, and soon found himself in the hall of which his pretended uncle had spoken.

Not taking any notice of the great vases of gold and silver on every side, he went quickly through the three halls, being very careful not to touch the walls, even with his clothes, for fear he should die. When he came to the garden, he walked along the path until he reached the five steps, at the top of which he saw an old lamp burning in a niche.

He took it down, put out the light, emptied the liquid, and hid the lamp safely in his clothes. He then took a good look at the garden, in which he found trees laden with the largest and most beautiful fruits he had ever seen, some of which were white, some clear as crystal, and others red, green, blue, purple, or yellow.

Now, these fruits were really diamonds, rubies, pearls, emeralds, sapphires, and other precious stones. But Aladdin, having no idea of their great value, thought they were only made of coloured glass; yet, being pleased with their beauty, he thought he might as well take some of them home with him. So he quickly filled all his pockets, and the two new purses his uncle had given him, and even stuffed his loose clothes quite full of the pretty fruits; and then, loaded with riches, of the value of which he had no idea, he returned through the three halls with great care, and ran up the steps to the mouth of the little cave.

The magician, full of impatience, called down through the small opening for Aladdin to hand him up the lamp first of all, since it would be in his way as he scrambled through the hole; but Aladdin said the lamp did not trouble him, and he would give it up when he came above ground, if his uncle would lend him a hand to help him out of the hole.

This made the magician angry, and he said he must have

the lamp first before he helped him out; but Aladdin, having filled his clothes so full of the fruits, could not well get at it, and still refused to give it up until he got above ground.

The magician now flew into a most violent rage, and throwing some more incense into the fire above, he again uttered some magic words, which caused the stone to move back to its place on the top of the cave, and the ground to cover it over as before, so that poor Aladdin was thus buried alive.

This cruel act served to prove that this pretended uncle was no real relation of Aladdin, but as wicked a magician as any in the world. For a great number of years he had lived in Africa, that country of mystery and of wonders, where he had learnt all the magic and evil enchantments he could. Having found out that there was in the world a certain wonderful lamp, which, if he could only obtain it, would make him richer and more powerful than any king in the world, he made up his mind not to rest until he found it. By his enchantments he had lately learnt that the magic lamp lay hidden in a strange underground garden in a certain part of China, in exactly the place just described; and so had set off at once to the city which was nearest the great treasure that he wished to obtain.

Now, although he knew exactly where the lamp was, the magician learnt from his books that he was not allowed to take it himself, nor even to enter the underground garden, but that he must receive it from the hands of someone else. It was for this reason he had made friends with Aladdin, thinking that he was a lazy lad whose life was of no value, and meaning, when he had got the lamp from his hands, to bury him alive in the cave, that he might tell no tales.

However, the magician's own foolish impatience and hasty rage had spoilt his fine plans, and feeling that his hopes of obtaining the wonderful lamp were now gone for ever, since he had not the power to open the ground again, he quickly started back for Africa that same day. He was full of disappointment because he had failed to obtain his great wish, but he felt that at any rate Aladdin would not live to tell the story of what had happened, and this unkind thought comforted him a little.

However, there was one thing the bad magician had forgotten, and this was the magic ring he had placed on Aladdin's finger, which was now the means of saving the poor lad's life, as we shall see.

When Aladdin found himself shut up in the cave in complete darkness, and knew that he was buried alive, he was full of dismay and surprise, for he had never expected that his pretended uncle, after treating him so kindly, would play him such a cruel trick, and he called out that he was now ready to give up the lamp if his uncle would open the ground once more. But his cries were all in vain, since they could not be heard by anyone; and so the poor boy could do nothing but lie on the steps and weep in despair.

For two days he remained like this. Then, feeling that he would soon die, he clasped his hands together to pray for the last time, and in joining his hands he rubbed the ring given him by the magician, not knowing of the magic power it possessed.

But no sooner had he thus rubbed the ring than instantly there rose out of the ground before him an enormous genie, who said to him: "What wouldst thou have with me? I am ready to obey thee as thy slave, and the slave of all who possess the ring upon thy finger—I and the other slaves of the ring!"

At almost any other time the sight of a genie would have frightened Aladdin so much that he would have been unable to speak; but now the horror of being buried alive overcame all other fears, and he answered at once: "Whoever you are, get me out of this place, if you can."

Directly he had spoken these words, the earth opened and closed again, and he found himself alone in the open air once more, just in the very place where the magician had made the fire.

As soon as Aladdin had got over his surprise, he made up his mind to try and find his way home again. Although he had been brought so far out into the country by the magician, who he now knew could not have been his uncle, he was glad to find that he remembered quite well how they had come; and, having once made his way into the gardens, he soon reached the city, and went straight to his home.

Want of food, and joy at being safe home again, completely overcame poor Aladdin; but as soon as he was better, and had taken a little food, he told his mother of all the dreadful things that had happened to him, and showed her the old lamp and fruits he had taken out of the underground garden.

His mother had no more idea of the great value of the beautiful fruits than he had, but, like him, only thought they vere made of coloured glass. When Aladdin had put them carelessly behind the cushions of the sofa, to be out of the way, she eagerly listened to the rest of his story, for she was full of indignation at the cruel conduct of the false uncle, but glad that her boy, whom she really loved, had escaped from so wicked a magician.

When Aladdin had come to the end of his story, he was only too glad to go to rest, since he was very tired after his adventures; but on asking for some breakfast next morning he was grieved to learn that his poor mother had no food in the house. However, he told her not to be troubled, as he would take out the old lamp he had brought yesterday, and sell it; and they could buy at least a little food with the money he got for it.

His mother brought the lamp to him, and, seeing that it was very dirty, she said she would clean it up a bit; but no sooner had she started rubbing the lamp than a most hideous genie of the largest size suddenly appeared before her, and said in a loud voice: "What wouldst thou have? I am ready to obey thee as thy slave, and the slave of all who have that lamp in their hands—I and the other slaves of the lamp!"

The poor woman was so dreadfully frightened at the sight of the genie that she fainted; but Aladdin snatched the lamp out of her hand, and said: "I am hungry, bring me something to eat!"

The genie vanished, but instantly appeared again with a

large silver tray, on which were twelve covered silver plates full of the richest foods; and then, having also brought six large white loaves, two bottles of wine, and two silver cups, he placed the things on the floor and disappeared.

Aladdin now brought water, and, sprinkling a little on her face, brought his mother out of her faint; and then they both sat down to the splendid meal before them.

When Aladdin's mother presently learnt that it was the dreadful genie who had brought these fine things she felt very uneasy, and begged her son to be careful what he did, advising him to sell the lamp and the ring on his finger, and have nothing more to do with such magic things. But Aladdin told her that this would be a foolish thing to do, since they had already seen what wonders could be worked by means of these magic things; and he said he would certainly keep the lamp, though he would hide it out of his mother's sight, since she was afraid of it, and the ring he meant to wear always on his finger, to help him when he was in danger.

So his mother said nothing more, and Aladdin put the lamp in a safe place, where he could easily find it again and the ring he was careful to keep always on his finger.

When they had eaten all the food brought by the genie, Aladdin, determined not to suffer hunger any more, took one of the silver plates to a Jewish dealer, and asked him if he would buy it. The Jew, seeing at once that the plate was really of great value, was ready enough to buy it, and offered a gold piece in exchange for it. Aladdin went away quite satisfied, having no idea that the plate was really worth very much more.

He bought food with the money, and when this was finished he took another silver plate to the Jew, who paid him the same price again.

By this means the poor widow and her son, with care, were able to live in some comfort; and now a great change for the better took place in Aladdin. His late strange adventures had the effect of changing him from a lazy, careless lad into a steady, sensible young man. He left off idling his time away with bad companions, and began, instead, to speak with merchants and learned men, gleaning all he could from their talk and ways. By noticing how they conducted their business, he thus gained some knowledge of the world. Being by nature bright and clever, he soon began to improve very much, and in a short time no one could have recognized in him the idle, good-for-nothing lad whom the cunning magician had chosen out to serve his evil purposes.

When Aladdin had sold all the plates, and even the great silver tray brought by the genie, and when the money he got for them was used up, he took the magic lamp once more, and rubbed it. Instantly the genie appeared, and asked what he desired; and upon Aladdin saying he was hungry, the hideous monster again brought him a silver tray full of dishes of food as before. When the food was finished Aladdin took the silver dishes, one by or.e, to be sold; but this time he met with one of the best goldsmiths in the city, who gave him sixty pieces of silver for each, which was their real value.

With this money Aladdin and his mother kept themselves comfortably for quite a long time, though they still lived in a very plain way. By talking with merchants and jewellers Aladdin soon learnt another very surprising thing; he discovered that the beautiful fruits which he had taken out of the underground garden were not made of coloured glass, as he had supposed, but were really precious jewels of untold value. But, though he was full of joy at this discovery, he kept it secret, even from his mother, at first.

It was just at this time that Aladdin first saw the sultan's daughter, the beautiful Princess Badroulbadour, and fell in love with her. Now, it was quite against the law for any ordinary person to look upon the face of the princess; but Aladdin, hearing that she would pass by a certain part of the city one day, when everyone was expected to be out of the way, hid himself behind a door, and managed to get a glimpse of her. He was so delighted with her great beauty that he loved her at once, and felt he could never be happy unless he married her.

When he told his mother of this she only laughed at him, and said he was foolish even to dream of such a thing, for the sultan would certainly never allow his daughter to be married to the son of a poor tailor. But Aladdin said he had quite made up his mind to marry the beautiful princess, and he begged his mother so hard to help him that at last she agreed to do so. So when Aladdin brought out the pretty fruits he had gathered in the underground garden, and told her that he had found out lately that they were really priceless jewels, and desired her to take them as a gift to the sultan, at the same time asking the hand of the Princess Badroulbadour in marriage, she said she would do so, and placing the jewels in a great china dish, she set out for the palace.

After some trouble she managed to get into the great hall where the sultan was dealing out justice to those who brought complaints before him; but everybody was too busy to take any notice of her. The next day she went again, but met with no better luck; and it was not until she had visited the palace for six days that the sultan, who had noticed the poor woman standing in the same place so patiently during this time, at last commanded that she should be brought up to the throne.

When Aladdin's mother came up to the throne she bowed low before the sultan, and humbly begged him to listen to what she had to say. She then told of the love that Aladdin had for the Princess Badroulbadour, and how greatly he desired to marry her, and at the same time she presented the sultan with the dish of jewel-fruits that she had brought.

The sultan was so pleased with the dazzling beauty of these priceless gems that, far from being angry with the poor widow for daring to ask such a thing of him, he said that he would surely do well to give his daughter to a man who valued her at so high a price; but his grand vizier, who stood close at hand, advised him not to act too hastily. As it happened, the sultan had already half-promised his daughter to the grand vizier's son; and so the minister now reminded him of this, asking him to wait three months longer before settling the matter, when his son would most likely be able to bring a more noble present even than that of Aladdin, who was an entire stranger.

The sultan agreed to this, and told Aladdin's mother to go home and tell her son that he accepted his offer, but could not let the princess be married until some special furniture was got ready for her, which would be finished in three months' time.

Aladdin was full of joy when he heard this good news, and was most eager for his wedding-day to come. But he soon learnt that the sultan did not mean to keep his promise. One day his mother came rushing into the house, telling him that the streets were all decorated, and, upon asking the reason, she had just learnt that it was because the Princess Badroulbadour was to be married that very night to the grand vizier's son.

This was a terrible disappointment for Aladdin, but still he was not without hope of getting the princess for himself after all, and as soon as his mother had gone out of the room he took the magic lamp and rubbed it hard. As before, the genie appeared instantly, and asked what he desired. Aladdin explained how unfairly he had been treated by the sultan, and then he desired the genie to help him by bringing the royal bride and bridegroom to his house that night. The genie promised to do so, and Aladdin felt satisfied.

The wedding rejoicings went on all the evening, but no sooner had the princess and the vizier's son retired to rest in the palace, than the genie appeared, and, raising the royal couch on to his shoulders, flew with it in an instant to Aladdin's house, where the princess was left in a dark room by herself, and the poor bridegroom was locked up in a cold, dismal cellar all night.

When morning came they were taken back to the palace in the same astonishing manner, and as the whole adventure seemed like a dreadful dream, neither the princess nor the vizier s son said anything about it to the sultan.

When, however, the same thing happened again next night, they were both so much alarmed that they dared not keep the matter a secret any longer. The vizier's son, seeing that magic was at work, said he would rather give up his bride than go through such a night again, and be the means of bringing trouble upon the princess.

On hearing what had taken place, the sultan, agreeing with the vizier's son, at once ordered all the wedding rejoicings to be stopped, and the marriage declared not to have taken place. Aladdin was full of joy to find how well his plan had worked, and to know that the beautiful princess was once more free to become his own bride.

However, he waited till the three months the sultan had asked were over, and then he sent his mother once more to the palace to ask again for the princess's hand in marriage.

The sultan at once recognized the widow, and listened quietly to what she had to say; but as the grand vizier again advised him to take time, he told her that Aladdin should only marry his daughter on condition that he sent him first as a present forty golden basins full of the same sort of priceless jewels he had sent before, carried by forty black slaves led by the same number of handsome white slaves, all of whom were to be richly dressed!

The widow went sadly home, feeling sure that her son would now have to give up all idea of marrying the princess, since he would nevei be able to send such a present to the sultan. But Aladdin did not lose hope, and as soon as his mother left him he rubbed his wonderful lamp, and the genie again stood before him.

He quickly explained what he wanted as a gift for the sultan, and in a very short time the genie returned with forty splendidly-dressed handsome white slaves, followed by forty black slaves, bearing on their heads solid golden basins full of diamonds, pearls, rubies, emeralds, and other precious stones, all of which were even larger and more beautiful than those taken from the underground garden.

The slaves quite filled Aladdin's little house and garden. When it had learnt that nothing more was wanted, the genie vanished.

Aladdin was quite delighted, and sent the slaves at once to the palace, persuading his mother to follow in their train, to present them to the sultan in his name.

When the slaves arrived at the palace they made a great stir, for none of the lords or ladies had ever before beheld such splendid servants; and when the sultan saw the golden basins full of dazzling jewels, which they laid at his feet, he was delighted, and felt that he could not do better than give his daughter to so rich a suitor.

So he told Aladdin's mother that her son should now certainly marry the princess, and that the sooner he came to fetch her the better he would be pleased.

Quickly the widow hurried back home with this good news, and Aladdin once more took his magic lamp and brought the genie before him. This time he asked the genie to dress him in rich clothes, fit for the most splendid king, and to bring him the finest horse in the world to ride upon, with twenty slaves to go before him, and twenty slaves to follow him, all as richly clothed as those he had sent to the sultan. Besides this, he ordered that six gaily-dressed female slaves, each carrying gorgeous robes fit for a queen, should be brought for his mother; and he also asked the genie to leave him ten thousand pieces of gold in ten purses.

When all these things had been brought, and the genie had vanished, Aladdin, dressed magnificently and looking like a handsome young prince on his prancing horse, set off for the palace, with his mother and the slaves following in a grand procession. As he thus rode along in state, he gave orders to certain of the slaves to throw showers of gold pieces amongst the crowds of people who stood in the streets to watch him go by.

In this splendid manner, followed by the cheers of the crowd, Aladdin arrived at the palace, where he was received as a prince by the sultan, who was now ready for the marriage to take place that very day.

But Aladdin said he could not think of taking the Princess Badroulbadour away from her father until he had built a splendid palace for her to live in; and he asked the sultan to allow him a space to set up such a building, within sight of his own palace.

To this the sultan gladly agreed, and, after a most splendid feast, Aladdin returned to his home, where he quickly called the genie of the lamp to his aid once more.

He now asked the genie to build, opposite to that of the sultan, a magnificent palace, the walls of which were to be made of solid gold and silver, and the windows, doors, and pillars of which were to be decorated and covered with pearls, diamonds, rubies, and every kind of precious stone. The inside was to be furnished in the most gorgeous style. Slaves, lords, and ladies, all splendidly dressed, were to be ready to wait in every room. A great treasure of gold and silver was to be laid in a certain secret part, known to Aladdin only, who also told the genie to be sure to leave one of the large jewelled windows unfinished.

Having thus given his orders, Aladdin went to bed. When he awoke next morning he found that the genie had indeed caused a wonderful palace, even more gorgeous than anything he could ever have imagined, to be built for him in the place he had named; and he and his mother at once took up their abode there.

When the sultan beheld from his own windows this dazzling palace, sparkling and glittering in the sunlight with priceless jewels and fine gold, he was amazed and delighted beyond measure. On that very evening the marriage of his daughter with Aladdin took place in splendid state, and the greatest rejoicings were held in the city.

Next day the sultan himself entered the jewel-palace, to admire it more closely, and then it was that he noticed that one of the windows had been left unfinished. When he asked the reason of this, Aladdin said that this had been done by his orders, as he wished to give the sultan the pleasure of putting the finishing touch to the wonderful palace himself.

The sultan was pleased with the idea, and at once sent for his chief jewellers, bidding them finish the window with gems in the same manner as the others in the palace.

The jewellers set to work without delay, but, though they did their best, at the end of a month the window was not half-finished, and they were at a standstill for want of jewels, having used up all that the sultan and even his grand vizier had.

Then Aladdin, who had known all along that their work would be in vain, and had only wished to prove still further that he was even richer and more powerful than the sultan himself, ordered the jewellers to undo their work, and take their jewels away again. He then called the genie into his presence, and desired him to finish the window in the same manner as the others. This was done instantly; and when the sultan saw this fresh proof of Aladdin's power, he was more pleased with him than ever.

Now that Aladdin had gained the very height of his wishes, being married to the beautiful Princess Badroulbadour, and living the life of a splendid prince, he was perfectly happy. But after a while trouble once more came upon him.

The wicked magician was still alive, and having learnt by means of his magic that Aladdin had not died in the cave, but was living happily the life of a prince, and still had the wonderful lamp in his keeping he became very angry and jealous. After a while he made up his mind to go back to China and try once more to get the magic lamp for himself, and, if possible, to destroy Aladdin's happiness. So he set off, and soon arrived in the city where Aladdin lived. In a very short time he found out all he could about his doings and the wonderful power that he had in the land.

Having learnt that Aladdin himself was at present away hunting in the country he thought of a cunning plan for stealing the magic lamp before he came back. Dressing himself up as a poor merchant, he bought a basket full of small lamps, and then went from street to street, calling out:

"New lamps for old lamps! Who will change old lamps for new ones?"

Even the children in the streets laughed at him for making such a foolish offer; but the magician heeded them not, and soon came crying his wares before the dazzling windows of Aladdin's splendid palace.

It happened that one of the princess's ladies noticed him, and going at once to her mistress she said: "There is a foolish fellow outside who says he will give new lamps in exchange for old ones! I have seen in Prince Aladdin's room a dirty old lamp that can surely be of no use. Shall I take it down to the merchant and ask him to give me a new one for it?"

The Princess Badroulbadour, having no idea of the real value of the magic lamp, laughed, and said she might do so if she chose; so the lady-in-waiting took the old lamp down to the pretended merchant, who eagerly grabbed it, and gave her a fine new one in exchange for it.

No sooner had the magician left the palace, and made his way to a lonely spot, than, seeing that the lamp was indeed the one he sought, he rubbed it hard, and the genie instantly appeared, ready to obey him as the owner of the lamp. To him the magician said: "Carry me, together with Aladdin's palace, with the princess and all within it, into the middle of Africa!" These words were hardly spoken when the genie obeyed them to the letter, and in an instant the magician and Aladdin's palace were set down in a lonely plain in the heart of Africa.

Next morning, •vhen the sultan arose, he was astonished and terribly upset to find that the dazzling jewel-palace, with his beloved daughter and all within it, had entirely vanished. Full of rage and grief he sent soldiers to meet Aladdin on his return from hunting, and had him brought as a captive before him.

Aladdin was even more shocked and grieved at what had

happened than the sultan, who was eager to have him be-headed at once. His great love for the princess made Aladdin hope that he might yet save her from danger, and he begged the sultan to allow him forty days in which to search for her. If at the end of that time he should meet with no success, he would gladly give up his life.

The sultan agreed to this, and Aladdin began his search; but he seemed so dazed and helpless that he could scarcely think, and many people began to look upon him as mad. After rushing wildly about the city for several days, searching in vain for the princess and for news of his palace, poor Aladdin wandered out into the country, where he flung himself down on the bank of a river, in the utmost grief, feeling that his task was quite hopeless, and that he might as well drown himself.

He was just about to say his prayers for the last time when he suddenly slipped down the bank, and in grasping hold of a rock to save himself he happened to rub the magic ring which the magician had given him, and which he had worn on his finger so constantly that he had forgotten about its powers for the time being. However, he found it of great service now; for no sooner had he rubbed it against the rock than there appeared the same genie as he had seen in the cave, who at once asked for his commands.

Very pleasantly surprised, Aladdin asked for his palace to be brought back to its place in the city. But the genie said he could not quite do this, since that power belonged only to the genie of the lamp; so Aladdin asked instead to be set down beneath the window of the princess's room in the palace wherever it might be.

In an instant Aladdin found himself in the midst of a lonely plain in Africa, standing outside his own splendid palace.

It was night when he arrived; but early in the morning the Princess Badroulbadour looked out of her window, and seeing Aladdin outside in the garden, she was full of delight, and sent for him to be brought to her at once.

Aladdin was overjoyed to find himself with his beautiful

princess once more, and he quickly asked her to tell him all she knew of the dreadful thing that had happened to them both, and also if she knew what had become of the old lamp which he kept in his own room. The princess explained how she had allowed the old lamp to be exchanged for a new one, and was greatly surprised now to learn of its real value. She also stated how frightened she had been on waking up to find herself so suddenly in Africa, and far away from anyone's help.

Aladdin next asked for news of the magician, who he now knew had played him this trick, and the princess said that the wicked sorcerer came to see her once every day, being eager to marry her himself, but that she always treated him with such scorn that he did not care to come oftener.

Aladdin now thought out a careful plan; and on learning that the magician carried the lamp about with him, hidden in his clothes, he told the princess to overcome her dislike so far as to invite the sorcerer to have supper with her that night, and to give him a cup of wine in which a certain poison should be mixed.

The princess gladly agreed to do this, and sent an invitation at once to the magician to come to supper with her that night, whilst Aladdin quickly made his way to the nearest city, where he bought a deadly drug, and returned with it to the palace. He mixed the poison in a cup of wine, which he told the princess to entice the magician to drink during supper-time; and then he hid himself in another room to await the end of his plan.

The magician came in good time to the supper, and was quite delighted to find the princess beautifully dressed, and waiting with smiles to receive him. They sat down to quite a splendid feast, and talked and laughed together in the most friendly manner; and when the princess at last offered the magician the cup of poisoned wine, he drank it off without any fear, as he had done the other wine before. But no sooner had the wicked sorcerer taken that deadly drink than he fell over on the couch quite lifeless.

Aladdin now rushed into the room, and searching amongst the dead magician's clothes, to his joy he found the magic lamp, and then, quickly rubbing it, he brought the genie before him, and desired that the palace should be set down in its proper place in China once again.

This was instantly done, and you can imagine the surprise and the joy of the sultan when he again set eyes on Aladdin's palace, and knew that his dear daughter was still alive and safe within.

The greatest rejoicings were kept up all over the country for a very long time, in honour of the return of the princess. But even now Aladdin was not out of danger.

It happened that the African magician had a younger brother, who had also studied magic, and who, having learnt by his arts what had happened to his brother, at once set off for China to take revenge on Aladdin.

Having arrived in the city, he soon thought out a clever plan; and hearing of a certain holy woman, named Fatima, whose goodness had caused her to be much respected and beloved by the people, he went to the cell where she lived all alone. Here he very soon killed poor Fatima, buried her, and dressed himself up in her clothes. Then he stained his face and eyebrows exactly to look like the colour of hers and walked out into the city passing himself off as the holy woman.

His disguise was so good that everybody thought him to be the holy woman, and followed him in crowds begging his blessing. at length he came to the palace, and the princess, hearing of that Fatima was in the street, sent her slaves to ask the holy woman into the palace.

The princess, having heard much about the holy woman, begged the pretended Fatima to remain in the palace, that she might learn from her how to be truly good. This was settled; and later the princess took her new friend into the splendid hall of the palace, and asked her what she thought of it.

The false Fatima said it was truly noble, and needed but one thing to make it the most splendid hall in the world; and

when asked by the princess to name this thing, she said that
if a roc's egg were hung up in the golden dome it would, indeed, be quite perfect.

The wicked magician said this because he knew that if
Aladdin asked for a roc's egg, the genie would be very angry, and would most likely kill him, for the roc was a magic
bird, and served by genii; but the princess did not know
this, and when next she saw Aladdin she asked him to order
that a roc's egg should be hung up in the hall.

So Aladdin rubbed the magic lamp, and commanded the
genie to hang a roc's egg up in the golden dome; but on
hearing this the genie flew into a great rage, saying that
Aladdin deserved to be destroyed for asking such a thing,
after all that had already been done for him.

Aladdin was much alarmed, for he did not even know
what a roc was; but the genie, seeing that he had not really
meant to offend him, explained that the so-called holy
woman was really the magician's brother, and advised
Aladdin to be on his guard.

Aladdin was, however, not long in thinking of a way to
get rid of his enemy. So, when the genie had vanished,
Aladdin went to the princess's room, where, pretending to
have a bad headache, he caused the holy woman to be sent
for, to see if she could cure it.

The Princess, delighted with the idea of being able to cure
her husband, said that the good Fatima was in the building
and ran to fetch her.

The false Fatima came with one hand lifted up as if to
bless Aladdin while with the other she grasped a dagger
hidden in the folds of her cloak. No sooner, however, did
she draw near him than Aladdin seized his dagger and
stabbed her, so that she fell down dead.

The princess was at first shocked that her husband had
killed the holy woman; but Aladdin, pulling off the hood of
the dead woman's cloak, soon explained to her his reason,
and showed how she was really the African magician's
wicked brother, who had meant to kill them both.

The grief of the princess was then turned to joy as she realised there was no more danger to be feared, and Aladdin and his beautiful princess settled down to live in happiness and splendour; and when at length the sultan of China died, Aladdin and his beautiful wife reigned together in peace for the rest of their lives, and left behind them many good and beautiful children.

Beder and Giauhara

There was once a King of Persia who had gained so many glorious victories, and conquered so many countries, that he had made himself the richest and most powerful monarch in the world, and was called by the proud title of "King of Kings". He had many beautiful wives, and every rich treasure that he could desire, and he would have been perfectly happy but for one thing. He had no son to reign after him, and it often made him sad to think that the power and the glory that he had gained would never be enjoyed by a child of his. He gave large sums of money and rich gifts to the holy men of the country in the hope that their prayers might gain for him his great desire, but the years went on and still no prince was born.

However, one day there came to the court a merchant from a distant land, who brought with him a beautiful slave-maiden, whom he wished to sell to the king. The merchant was at once taken into the splendid hall, where the King of Persia was going through the duties of the day with his great lords, and when the council was at an end the king called him forward and asked him his business.

The merchant bowed low before the throne, and said that he had brought with him a slave-maiden so wonderfully beautiful and gifted that he felt sure even so great a king could never have seen her equal.

The King of Persia said he should like to see her, and he went at once into the room where the fair slave had been left. When the merchant had lifted the veil from his slave the king saw before him a lady so wonderfully beautiful that he at once fell in love with her, and wished to have her for his wife. He said that he would pay ten thousand pieces of gold for the slave, and the merchant went away well satisfied.

The beautiful slave was taken into a splendid room, the windows of which overlooked the sea, and the king ordered the other women-slaves and nurses to wait upon her, and dress her in the most gorgeous robes and jewels that could be obtained.

When next the king came to see her the lovely slave was sitting on a sofa near the window that overlooked the sea, and when he entered she merely turned her head to see who it was, and then took no further notice of him. The King of Persia was much surprised that she did not rise to receive him in a proper manner, but he went up to the window at once and tried to make friends with her.

However he found this no easy task, for though he spoke to her for a long time, admiring her beauty and telling her over and over again how greatly he loved her, she would not answer him, and nothing that he could say would make her look at him or cause her to utter a single word.

The king was much grieved at this strange conduct, but, hoping that a little gaiety would change her sadness into content, he ordered a fine feast to be brought into the room, and a lively entertainment of merry music and dancing to take place at once.

But, although the beautiful slave ate at the feast and allowed the king to admire and talk to her as much as he pleased, she still would not speak a word herself, but kept her eyes fixed on the ground, and she took no notice whatever of the dancing and the music.

The king, fearing now that his new slave was dumb, asked the attendant ladies and slaves if they had yet heard her speak, and the attendants answered that though they had praised her beauty, and asked her wishes in the matter of her robe's and jewels, she had not replied, nor uttered a single word.

The King of Persia felt sad on hearing this, but by this time he had grown to love the beautiful slave so dearly that, dumb or not, he determined to make her his queen. He set aside a splendid suite of rooms for her, and ordered a great number of slaves to attend her.

But, although the King of Persia did all in his power to please her, for a whole year the beautiful strange lady did not utter a single word to him. At the end of the year, as he sat beside her one day, he said: "My queen, I love you more than ever! Although it is now a year since I made you my queen, I have never felt regret for the act, and I should be perfectly happy if you would but speak to me. I feel sure that you are not really dumb, and if only you will give me the joy of hearing you utter one single word I do not care, after that, how soon I die!"

On hearing this the beautiful slave smiled, and then, to the great joy of the king, she began to speak to him. She thanked him for his kindness to her, and said she had grown to love him very dearly, and the king was so delighted to know that she was not dumb after all that he gave orders to his lords to send large sums of money to the poor, to show how thankful he was that the queen had spoken at last.

He then begged the fair slave to tell him her story, and the reason why she had kept silent for so long a time. The strange lady now spoke readily enough, and she first told the king that her reason for not behaving as an ordinary slave was that she was really a royal princess, whose sadness was caused by the loss of her country and her friends.

"I am an ocean-princess," she said, "and my name is Gulnare of the Sea! My father, who is now dead, was one of the most powerful kings of the sea, and when he died he left his kingdom to my brother, Saleb, and my mother, Queen Farasche. We were all very happy together until the grasping ruler of a neighbouring country, envious of our pleasant land, came with a mighty army, and made himself master of it. We had only just time to escape with a few attendants to a safe hiding-place, and here my brother had to make his plans for driving away our enemies. He was so afraid harm should happen to me whilst matters were so upset that he wished to see me married at once. As our misfortunes prevented him from arranging a marriage with one of our own sea-princes just then, he hoped I would be willing to wed a prince of the earth; but this made me very angry, for we sea-folk are a proud race, and think it beneath us to wed with the families of the earth.

"It was in vain for my brother to point out that such an act would now be for my good, and at last I grew so displeased with him that I gave a great spring from the bottom of the sea up into the Island of the Moon.

"Here I was soon found by a certain rich lord, who, finding that I was too proud to make friends with him, sold me to the slave-merchant from whom Your Majesty bought me. I did not mean to remain with you, and had you not treated me with such kindness and respect I should soon have plunged into the sea from this window; and it was in order to prove your patient goodness and love that I chose to keep silence for a year."

The King of Persia was amazed at the strange story told him by his queen, and he now asked her to tell him something of the sea-folk, since he could not understand how they could live in the water without being drowned.

Queen Gulnare then explained that her people were so formed that they could breathe either in the sea or on land, and that the water did not even wet their clothes. She then went on to tell him of the vast countries of the ocean, and of the fine cities and mighty nations they contained; and she also described the untold riches of the sea, saying that the jewels and pearls there were all of far greater size and dazzling beauty than even the largest and most splendid found on earth.

After telling the king many other interesting things, Queen Gulnare ended her story by asking him to allow her to send for her mother, brother, and cousins, whom she longed to see again; and she added that they would be delighted to know that she was married to so mighty a ruler as the King of Persia.

The King of Persia said he would be delighted to receive Queen Farasche and King Saleb, though he did not know how a message could be sent to them in the sea; but Queen Gulnare said she could bring them to the palace in a moment, and if the king would but step into a cupboard close by, and look through a grating there, he should see the manner of their arrival.

The King of Persia went into the cupboard at once, and then Queen Gulnare made one of her slaves fetch a little fire in a fire-pan. When she was left alone she put a piece of aloes into the fire-pan, and as the smoke arose she uttered some strange words not known to the King of Persia, who, looking through the grating, saw beyond the open window that the sea began to be much disturbed.

Presently the sea opened, and a tall, noble-looking young man rose out of it, followed by a queenly lady advanced in years, who was attended by five lovely young maidens. When they came to the edge of the sea they all sprang lightly in at the palace window, and the King of Persia saw that, though they had only just come from the sea, their clothes were not wet, and that the whole party shone with dazzling brightness and were as beautiful as the dawn.

Queen Gulnare kissed her mother and brother many times, and when they had rejoiced together for some minutes she told them the whole story of her adventures since she had left the sea. King Saleb and Queen Farasche were delighted to know that she was now Queen of Persia and wife of the most powerful ruler on earth, and they asked her if she was happy and contented to remain on land, and Queen Gulnare said she now loved the King of Persia so dearly that she would never leave him, for she was perfectly happy as his wife.

The hidden King of Persia was overjoyed to hear this, and

when Queen Gulnare called him forward to be presented to her relations, he received them with every mark of honour. He invited them to stay some time in his palace, and every day he entertained them with fine shows and magnificent feasts.

Towards the end of their visit a beautiful baby prince was born to the King and Queen of Persia, and this happy event added to the joy of the whole party. The greatest rejoicings were held all over the country, and the royal baby was named Beder, which means Full Moon.

One day, when the royal party were all talking together, the nurse entered the room with the little prince in her arms. King Saleb at once arose, and, taking the baby up, began to fondle and toss him about in great delight; and then, without a word of warning, he sprang with him through the open window, and plunged into the sea.

The King of Persia gave a cry of dismay, expecting that his little son would be drowned; but Queen Gulnare said there was no fear, for the baby prince, like herself, could live equally well in the sea and on the land. And, sure enough, in a short time King Saleb returned with the little prince, as lively as ever, and both perfectly dry. The sea-king then presented to the King of Persia a splendid box of jewels which he had been to fetch. There were three hundred diamonds as large as pigeons' eggs, three hundred huge rubies, three hundred emerald wands, each six inches long, and thirty strings of enormous pearls, each string ten feet in length. The King of Persia was amazed at the sight of such dazzling jewels, but Queen Gulnare told him that they were as nothing compared with the other great riches and treasures of the ocean.

Soon after this the royal sea-folk returned to their own country beneath the waves, promising to return again from time to time; and the Court of Persia once more settled down to its usual daily customs.

Prince Beder was brought up with the greatest of loving care, and, being handsome, clever, brave, and amiable, he grew to be the most delightful young prince of his time.

When he was only fifteen years of age, his father, feeling that he was now growing old, determined to make his son king in his place, and as his chief viziers and all the people were also willing, Prince Beder was crowned King of Persia amidst great rejoicings.

The new king, young though he was, soon proved himself to be a wise and clever ruler; and during the second year of his reign he visited all the chief cities in his kingdom, that he might see for himself that his people were happy and contented.

Soon after his return from this long journey his father became very ill and died. King Beder and his mother, Queen Gulnare, were in great grief for a long time, but at last the young king laid aside his mourning, and returned to his many duties again.

About a year later King Saleb found time to leave his kingdom beneath the sea for a while, and, having at last driven away all his enemies, he came to visit his relations on the land. One evening, as they were all talking together, King Saleb began to praise his nephew so highly, for the wise manner in which he ruled, that young King Beder, modestly not caring to hear himself so well spoken of, at last turned aside, and, lying back amongst his cushions, pretended to fall asleep.

King Saleb still continued his praises, and presently he said: "Sister, I wonder you have not thought of arranging a suitable marriage for your son. A handsome young prince of his age ought certainly to be married, and I must look for some beautiful princess of the sea who shall be worthy of him."

"You are right, my brother," replied Queen Gulnare; "but my son shows no desire to be married. Yet I like the idea of his marrying one of our own sea-princesses, and I wish you could find one so exceedingly beautiful that my son cannot fail to love her."

"I know of such a one!" said King Saleb. "Her name is Princess Giauhara, and she is the daughter of the King of Samandal, one of the most powerful rulers beneath the waves. But, unhappily, this king is so haughty and vain that he looks upon all other princes as far beneath him, and he is hardly likely to allow his daughter, who is the loveliest maiden in the sea, to enter our family, noble though we know it to be. But I will go myself and request his daughter as a bride for my nephew, the most powerful king on earth; and if he refuses, we must seek elsewhere for a princess. For this reason it is well King Beder should know nothing of our plans at present, for it would be sad if he should grow to love the Princess Giauhara and then be refused as a suitor by her haughty father. Therefore he must not see her until we get the consent of the King of Samandal."

After thus settling the matter, King Saleb and his sister began to talk of other matters, and presently King Beder pretended to awake. Now, he had heard every word that had been spoken, and he was so struck with the thought of the beautiful Princess Giauhara that he longed above all things to marry her, and felt that he loved her already.

He passed a restless night, and in the morning he invited his uncle, who was to return to the sea next day, to go hunting with him, meaning to tell him that he knew of his plans. King Saleb gladly accepted his invitation, and during the hunt King Beder told out his secret, and begged his uncle to take him also to ask for the hand of Princess Giauhara, saying that he already felt so much love for this beautiful lady that he would rather die than live longer without her.

On hearing these wild words King Saleb was much upset, and told his nephew that he could not take him away from Persia without the consent of his mother.

However, Beder declared that Queen Gulnare would never agree to part with him, and he begged his uncle so hard to take him away at once, without returning to the palace, or he should certainly die of grief, that King Saleb at last agreed to do so. He then gave his nephew a ring, telling him it would protect him from the dangers of the sea-depths; and when King Beder had placed the ring on his finger, they both mounted gracefully into the air towards the sea, and soon plunged in the waves.

In a very short time they arrived at the sea-king's beautiful palace, where they were both received with great joy by Queen Farasche, who, however, blamed her son for having allowed King Beder to know of their plans for him, since it was so doubtful whether they would ever come to a successful issue. But King Saleb soon explained to her how his nephew had overheard the talk between Queen Gulnare and himself; and so they agreed to make the best of the matter. They arranged that King Saleb should take a splendid present of jewels, and go himself to the King of Samandal to ask for his daughter's hand in marriage for King Beder, and Queen Farasche chose the present herself, which consisted of dazzling monster diamonds, rubies, emeralds, and pearls, in a handsome box.

Next morning King Saleb set off with a few attendants, and soon arrived at the palace of the King of Samandal. The haughty king received him with much honour, and seemed greatly pleased with the handsome gift he had brought; but when King Saleb asked for the Princess Giauhara's hand in marriage for his nephew, his pleasant manner soon changed.

King Saleb spoke very respectfully, stating how handsome, rich, powerful, and well-spoken-of King Beder was; but the proud, vain king only laughed scornfully, and said haughtily that he could not think of marrying his daughter into a family so much beneath his own.

King Saleb was greatly offended on hearing this, knowing that Beder's family was quite as noble and powerful as that of the boastful King of Samandal; but he still spoke quietly and again went on with the praises of his nephew. But what he said only made the King of Samandal more scornful and angry, and at last he flew into a violent rage, and ordered his guards to seize King Saleb, and cut off his head at once

But King Saleb was strong and active, and managed to escape from the guards before they had time to draw their swords; and, rushing towards the palace gates he was glad to find there about a thousand of his own soldiers and friends, whom Queen Farasche, thinking he might meet with bad treatment at the hands of the King of Samandal, had sent to his aid, soon after he had set off.

King Saleb now put himself at the head of this troop, and soon forced his way back through the palace guards to the room of the King of Samandal, whom he quickly made a prisoner.

He then went in search of the Princess Giauhara; but he could not find her, for the princess, on hearing the noise of fighting in the palace, had instantly sprung up from the bottom of the sea with her attendants, and escaped on to a desert island.

In the meanwhile some of the attendants who had set off with King Saleb, not having seen the soldiers who had soon afterwards come to the aid of their king, came rushing back to Queen Farasche with such alarming news of the King of Samandal's wild anger, that all were in fear for his safety. King Beder, feeling himself to be the cause of this trouble, and not knowing how he could set matters right, darted up from the bottom of the sea, and happened to land on the very island to which the Princess Giauhara had just come to escape danger.

He sat down to rest for a few moments; and, whilst he was thinking how he should act next, he heard voices close at hand, and looking around he saw a maiden so wonderfully beautiful that he felt at once she could be none other than the Princess Giauhara, who had evidently left her father's palace in fear. He went up at once to the place where she was standing with her attendants, and asked if he might help her in any way, since she seemed to be trouble.

The beautiful lady told him sadly that she was the Princess Giauhara, and that her father, the King of Samandal, had been suddenly seized by a certain King Saleb. She did not know why King Saleb had done this and she herself had only just had time to escape.

King Beder, glad to know that his uncle was safe and had

overcome the King of Samandal, now explained to the princess who he was, and how the commotion in her father's palace had come about; and, after telling her how greatly he already admired and loved her, he begged to be allowed to take her back home to obtain her father's consent to their marriage, which he felt the King of Samand would now give in return for his liberty.

But the Princess Giauhara, though she could not help admiring the handsome looks and charming manners of King Beder, was full of anger against him, feeling that she ought to regard him as an enemy, since he was the cause of her father's ill-treatment and her own fright an present trouble; and she made up her mind to escape from him as quickly as possible.

However, at first she pretended to receive him with great kindness, as though she would willingly become his bride; and she held out her hand in sign of friendship. But no sooner did King Beder take her hand in his, an joyfully stoop to kiss it, than she pushed him back; and throwing some water in his face, she cried: "Wretched man! take the form of a white bird with a red beak an red feet!"

In an instant King Beder was changed into just such a bird, and the princess bade one of her women take him at once to a dreadful place called the Dry Island, which was only a great ugly rock, where not a drop of water was to be had. However, the attendant had pity on poor King Beder, and, thinking that the princess, usually so kind and gentle, would later feel sorry for what she had done, she made up her mind to take him to a place where he could live in peace. So she took the bird to a pretty island, where people often came and went, and then she returned to her mistress.

Whilst King Beder was meeting with this unexpected treatment, King Saleb was still searching for the lost Princess Giauhara; but, failing to find her, he at last returned to his own palace, after having caused the King of Samandal to be shut up in a safe place, and given orders for the ruling of his newly-conquered kingdom. The first news he heard on his return home was of the disappearance of his nephew, and he sent out messengers in every direction to look for King Beder.

But the poor young King of Persia was nowhere to be found, and, whilst the search for him was still going on, King Saleb returned to rule for a while in the country of the King of Samandal, whom he still kept as a captive though treating him with proper respect.

Soon after this Queen Gulnare came to visit her mother, and to obtain news of her son, of whom she had heard nothing since the day he went hunting with King Saleb. On hearing from Queen Farasche the whole story of what had happened since the day of the hunting-party, and how King Beder had now utterly disappeared, Queen Gulnare was plunged in grief; but she was comforted a little by the thought that it was not certain her dear son was really lost for ever, and was wise enough to return to Persia at once, to save his kingdom for him.

She began to attend to the affairs of state herself, giving out that King Beder was staying for a while with his relations in the sea; and the people of Persia were satisfied with this explanation, and had no idea of the fears Queen Gulnare really had for the safety of her son. In the meantime poor King Beder was very unhappy in the island where he had been left in the form of a bird for he knew not how to find his way back to Persia, and even if he had known, it would have been useless to return since the people would not have been likely to acknowledge a white bird as their king. So he was obliged to stay where he was, feeding with other birds during the day and when night came choosing out the branch of a tree for his royal bed.

But one day a peasant came by with nets for snaring birds; and, seeing King Beder up in a tree, and thinking him a very handsome bird, he soon managed to get him into his net. Delighted with the prize he had gained the peasant put King Beder in a cage, and going straight to the royal palace he sold him to the king of the island for ten pieces of gold.

Later in the day, when the king was dining, he ordered the

cage to be brought before him, and took the bird out that he might admire it more closely; but, to his surprise the bird flew off his hand and began to peck at the bread and meats on the table. Thinking this very strange, the king sent for his queen to come and see the curious bird.

When the queen entered, and saw the bird, she at once covered her face with her veil; and on being asked by the king why she did so, she told him that the bird was not what it seemed to be, but was in reality a man.

"This bird", she said, "is King Beder of Persia, son of Queen Gulnare, and has been changed into a bird by the beautiful Princess Giauhara, daughter of the haughty King of Samandal". She then told the whole story of King Beder's late adventures; and since his queen was so clever in the art of magic that she knew of all things that were happening in every part of the world, the Island King knew she spoke the truth, and begged that she would restore the poor young king to his proper form again.

The queen gladly agreed to do so; and, sprinkling some water over the white bird, she uttered a few words of magic. No sooner had she spoken these words than the white bird vanished, and a handsome young prince stood in its place.

King Beder, delighted to find himself in his natural form once more, poured out his grateful thanks to the queen and then, turning to the king, and relating his story, he begged to be given the means of returning to Persia. The king gladly agreed to do so, and ordered one of his best ships to be set in order at once; and when it was ready King Beder set sail, after thanking his new friends for their kindness.

But alas for King Beder! A furious storm soon arose, and the ship was so violently tossed about by the waves that it struck on a rock, and went to pieces.

King Beder managed to cling to a piece of the wreck, and after much trouble he was able to reach the shore near to a large city. Here he found a great number of horses, camels, asses, cows, and other animals all crowding down to the beach, as though to prevent him from landing, and he had much difficulty in making his way through them.

At last he managed to escape from them, and entered the city; and, finding that the streets were almost deserted, he began to think the animals were right in trying to prevent him from entering, since it was perhaps dangerous to do so.

However, he went on till he came to a little fruit-shop, where he bid good-day to an old man sitting within. The old man asked him eagerly how he came to be there, and on hearing of the shipwreck he quickly brought King Beder inside the house, and set food before him.

King Beder was surprised at being so quickly hustled within; but he soon learned the reason of this. Whilst he was eating the old man told him that the place he had so unwisely entered was called the City of Enchantments, and that it was ruled by Queen Labe, a wicked sorceress, who though beautiful, was a most dangerous person to come across, since she had the power of changing people in animals. Whenever strange young men entered the city she had them brought before her, and for some days would show them great favour; but directly she grew tired of their company she would change them into the form of some animal or bird. King Beder now understood the kindness of the animals that tried to prevent him from entering the city, and he felt great pity for them on hearing that they were in reality human beings; and, full of dismay at having escaped one danger to fall into another, he told the old man his story, and who he really was.

The old man, whose name was Abdallah, now told King Beder that he meant to protect him, and he said that if the young man remained with him, and did not stray far from the house, all would be well, for he himself was greatly respected all over the city, and even by Queen Labe herself.

So King Beder thanked the old man for his kindness and gladly agreed to stay with him until he found a means of getting out of the City of Enchantments; and, as he was careful not to go away from the shop, he lived in safety for a while.

But one day, as he was sitting at the shop door, it happened that the sorceress, Queen Labe, came by with her attendants, and, noticing the handsome young stranger she stopped and asked Abdallah who he was. Abdalla said that the young man was his nephew, who had come to stay with him for a while; and then the sorceress having taken a sudden fancy to Beder, who was the handsomest young man she had ever seen, begged the old man to let his nephew come to her palace, that she might make him the most powerful person in the world. She begged so hard, promising that no harm should befall him, that a last Abdallah felt obliged to consent, though he declared he would not part with his nephew till the morrow; and Queen Labe then departed satisfied.

King Beder was greatly alarmed at the prospect before him; but Abdallah said he could save him from all harm. It appeared that the sorceress queen had no power over the old man, owing to certain powers of magic he himself had, which was the reason why she held him in such respect; nor would she dare to harm anyone belonging to him.

Next day Queen Labe came for King Beder; and when the young man had mounted the splendid horse she brought for him they rode back to the palace in great state.

At first Queen Labe treated her guest with the greatest honour and kindness, ordering delightful feasts and entertainments to take place every day; and she behaved so charmingly that he began to forget that she was a sorceress, and felt that he might enjoy her company without fear.

Forty days quickly passed by in this pleasant manner, and then Queen Labe made up her mind to treat King Beder as she had treated all the other guests she had ever brought to her palace.

On the fortieth night King Beder awoke suddenly, and saw that the magic queen was in his room, going through some strange performance, evidently thinking he was asleep. He saw her take in her hand a little box full of yellow powder, which she laid in a line across the floor. The powder instantly changed into a river of water, some of which the queen took up and mixed with flour in a basin. She kneaded this into a cake, with other magic powders, and then she baked it in a pan over the fire. She soon caused the little river to vanish by uttering certain magic words, and when the cake was ready she took it away, having no idea that King Beder had been watching her.

Amidst the delights of Queen Labe's court Beder had almost forgotten Abdallah, but now the danger he was in made him think of the good old man, who he felt could help him.

So next morning he begged Queen Labe to allow him to visit his uncle for a short time; and, having obtained her consent, he set off at once. Old Abdallah was overjoyed to see him, and when the young man told him of what he had seen the night before, he said all would be well if his directions were followed out.

He then gave Beder two cakes, and said: "When the sorceress asks you to eat some of her magic cake, do not refuse to take it; but when she is not looking break off part of one of my cakes, and eat that instead. When she thinks you have eaten her magic cake, she will throw water upon you, and try to change you into an animal; but of course she will not succeed. She will be terribly disappointed, but will try to pass the whole matter off as a joke. Then you must persuade her to eat some of the other cake I have given you, which is an enchanted one; and when she has done so, throw water in her face, and command her to take on any animal shape you desire. Thus shall the wicked sorceress get what she deserves, and suffer as she has caused others to suffer. Bring the animal to me, and I will then tell you what to do next."

King Beder returned at once to the palace with his two cakes. The harmless one he kept hidden in his pocket. The other he presented to Queen Labe, saying he had brought it from his uncle's table as a gift for her.

The magic queen said: "I will gladly eat it for your sake. But first let me beg of you to eat a piece of this, which I have made whilst you were away."

So saying she handed him the enchanted cake she had

made the night before. King Beder took the cake at once; but, changing it, unseen by the queen, for the one given him by old Abdallah, he began to eat that instead.

As soon as the wicked queen thought that Beder had eaten of her magic cake, she took a little water from stream close by, and said: "Wretch, quit the shape of man, and take on that of a lame and blind old horse!"

To her great surprise King Beder still remained unchanged, and so the queen, thinking she could not have made her magic cake aright, tried to pass the matter off as a joke, saying she had not meant to harm him.

King Beder now begged her to eat some of the cake he had given her, and the queen, wishing to restore his trust in her, and thinking the cake was just an ordinary one, at once broke off a piece and ate it. But no sooner had she done so than King Beder threw some water in her face and cried: "Wicked sorceress, be instantly changed into the shape of a mare!"

In a moment the queen was turned into a beautiful mare and King Beder led her along to Abdallah's house. The old man was delighted that all had turned out as he wished and that the wicked queen was punished as she deserved and he said to King Beder: "You may now mount the mare, my lord, and ride through the city in safety, to return to your own country. I have but one piece of advice to give you— do not sell the mare to anyone."

King Beder promised to remember; and, after thanking the old man for all his kindness, he joyfully mounted the mare, and set off on his journey, soon leaving the City of Enchantments far behind him.

Three days later he arrived in another great city, where he was stopped by an old man, who began to speak with him. Whilst they were talking, an old woman came up and began to weep bitterly at the sight of the mare, which she declared was exactly like one which her son had owned, but which was now dead. She then begged King Beder to sell the mare to her, or she and her son would die of grief.

Beder replied that his mare was not for sale, but added

that, even if she was, the old woman would scarcely be able to pay him a thousand pieces of gold, which was the smallest sum he would take for her.

But, to his surprise, the old woman said she would gladly pay that price, and Beder, not for a moment believing that one so poor-looking could find such a vast sum, said, in a joking way, that if the old woman could produce the thousand pieces of gold she should certainly have the mare.

To his utter astonishment the old woman at once counted out the sum he mentioned from a bag she had with her, and, much vexed, King Beder now told her he had only been joking, and did not mean to sell his mare for any price. But the old man with whom he had just been speaking now came forward and told him that, in the city where he now stood, if an agreement was once made it could not be broken or altered, and if he did not now sell the mare to the old woman, as he had agreed, some terrible misfortune would happen to him; King Beder was now sorry he had so rashly given his word; but since there was nothing else to be done he very unwillingly alighted.

Now the old woman who had thus tricked him was really the mother of Queen Labe, and had taught her all her magic, and no sooner had King Beder alighted than she seized the mare, and throwing some water in her face she cried "Dear daughter, take on your own shape again!" In an instant Queen Labe appeared, and then the old woman, by whistling, caused a gigantic genie to arise, who, taking up King Beder on one mighty shoulder, and the old woman and magic queen on the other, flew with them in a few moments to Queen Labe's palace in the City of Enchantments.

When they arrived there the magic queen turned upon King Beder in a frightful rage, and flinging water in his face she shrieked "Quit your own form again and take on that of an owl!"

In an instant poor King Beder was changed into an owl, and the wicked queen commanded one of her women to shut him up in a cage and give him neither food nor drink.

However, the attendant had pity on King Beder, and gave him both food and drink, and being also the friend of old Abdallah, she sent word to tell him how his nephew had been treated, that he might find some means of saving him.

Abdallah, having certain magic powers himself, at once called up a huge genie having four wings, who was named Lightning, and commanded him to take the kind attendant who had charge of King Beder in an instant to the royal palace of Persia, that she might tell Queen Gulnare of the danger in which her son was.

Lightning at once vanished, and suddenly appearing before Queen Labe's attendant, told her of Abdallah's plan, and then, lifting her to his shoulders, he flew with her in a few moments to Persia and set her down in the palace of Queen Gulnare.

The woman went straight to the royal rooms, where she found Queen Gulnare and Queen Farasche talking sadly together, and in a few words she told them of all that had happened to King Beder, and how he now needed their help.

The two queens received the kind attendant with great joy, delighted to know that their dear one was still alive, and they quickly made plans for the rescue of King Beder.

King Saleb was sent for without delay, and he soon called together his fierce sea-soldiers and the genii who were his friends.

When all the armies were ready he placed himself at their head, with the two queens and the kind attendant, and then the whole host rose into the air and swooped down upon the palace and City of Enchantments, so that the magic queen, her mother, and all who had joined in their wickedness were utterly destroyed in an instant.

Queen Gulnare then sent the attendant to fetch King Beder's cage from the place where she had left it, and when the woman returned with it she took out the owl, and, sprinkling water upon him, said: "My dear son, leave that strange shape and take on your own natural form again."

In a moment the owl vanished, and King Beder appeared,

and in great joy he rushed forward to embrace his loved ones.

After they had all rejoiced together for some time Queen Gulnare sent for old Abdallah, to thank him for his kindness to her son; and when asked what he wished to receive for a reward, the good man replied that he should like to marry the kind attendant he had sent to Persia, if she was willing, and then to serve King Beder for the rest of his life.

The attendant gladly consented, and Queen Gulnare promised that they should want for nothing.

By magic means King Saleb now called before them the King of Samandal, whom he had kept all this time a captive, though treating him with great honour, and directly he appeared King Beder threw himself at his feet, and asked him most respectfully once more for the honour of his daughter's hand in marriage.

The King of Samandal, whose haughty pride seemed to have at last left him, now gladly consented to the marriage, and he at once ordered some of his guards to go and look for his daughter. The Princess Giauhara was still in the island where the King of Persia had left her, and the guards soon brought her before her father.

The King of Samandal told her that he now wished her to marry the King of Persia, and Princess Giauhara, who had really loved King Beder from the first, said she would gladly marry him, since it was only duty to her father that had caused her to treat him unkindly before.

So Beder and Giauhara were married, amidst great rejoicings, in the City of Enchantments, and amongst the guests were the victims of the magic queen, who had returned to their natural forms at her death, all of them proving to be sons of kings and persons of high rank.

When the wedding rejoicings were over, King Saleb returned to the sea, where he soon restored the King of Samandal to his kingdom again, and King Beder set off for Persia in great joy, with his long-wished-for bride, the lovely Princess Giauhara.